BROTHERS IN BLOOD

DANIEL ST. JAMES

B
BERKLEY BOOKS, NEW YORK

BROTHERS IN BLOOD

A Berkley Book / published by arrangement with
the author

PRINTING HISTORY
Berkley edition / December 1991

ISBN: 0-425-13076-2

A BERKLEY BOOK ® TM 757, 375
Berkley Books are published by The Berkley Publishing Group,
200 Madison Avenue, New York, New York 10016.
The name "BERKLEY" and the "B" logo
are trademarks belonging to Berkley Publishing Corporation.

10 9 8 7 6 5 4 3 2 1

This novel is appreciatively
dedicated to my editor,
Gary Goldstein, whose ideas
and encouragement made this
book possible.

acknowledgments

In preparing for the *Brothers in Blood* saga, I read and drew upon *The Northwest Mounted Police* by J. P. Turner; *The Silent Force* by T. Morris Longstreth; the Time-Life Old West series; *The Royal Canadian Mounted Police* by Richard L. Nueberger; and novels by such excellent writers as Bill Pronzini, Dan Cushman, Terrance Dicks, Ian Anderson, William Byron Mowery, and Ottwell Binns.

April 2, 1887

SOMETIME AROUND MIDNIGHT, THE SENTRY heard a noise behind him. He turned, lowering his Snider carbine for quick use if necessary.

But it was too late.

The Indian was on him instantly, grabbing him around the neck and choking him so hard the sentry was forced to drop his carbine. The Indian then jerked a long knife from the belt he wore around his buckskin shirt, and slashed the edge of the knife across the sentry's throat.

Hot blood sprayed over the Indian's face.

He pushed the dead sentry facedown on the grass and then started toward the fort.

Fort Cree was a huge log structure located on the Cree River near the Canada-Montana border. It was run by the Royal Canadian Mounted Police, which had built it ten years earlier.

The sentry dead, the Indian had no trouble sneaking into the sleeping fort. His moccasins made his passage almost silent.

In the long shadows, the Indian saw the shapes of the various buildings, and the now-empty parade ground that stood in the center of the fort. At dawn a Union Jack would be run up the flagpole and flap proudly in the spring wind.

But the Indian's business would be over well before dawn, and the Indian long gone.

The officers' quarters were near the back of the vast fort. While the majority of the Mountie officers slept in the same long cabin, one man, Inspector Donald Adams, slept in a tiny cabin adjoining the other quarters. The fort's ranking officer always took this smaller residence.

It was the small cabin the Indian wanted.

He stood now in the shadows, looking back over the grounds to see if anybody else was about. From the stable he heard the sounds of a few restless horses but otherwise Fort Cree was silent.

The Indian slipped through the darkness to the cabin door, putting a large hand on the simple latch that held the door shut. After easing the latch upward with great care, the Indian went inside.

Inspector Adams slept with his head near the door. He lay bathed in moonlight, clothed in red long johns and sleeping faceup. He was an older man, with thinning white hair and white muttonchop sideburns. He made soft, wet snoring sounds.

The room smelled of sleep and pipe tobacco.

The Indian leaned in, clamped his hand over the inspector's mouth, and then raised his knife. It was still sticky with blood from killing the sentry.

Just before the Indian slashed the inspector's throat, the Mountie officer came awake and grabbed the Indian's wrist with bone-crushing force. The Indian was startled by the man's strength but somehow he held on and lowered the knife to the man's face. The Mountie struggled but it was too late.

Just before he died, however, Inspector Adams saw that his assassin was no Indian at all but in fact a white outlaw named Barton Jaeger, the area's most successful and ruthless whiskey runner. Jaeger would no doubt leave some Indian artifact behind so that the Mounties would blame the Cree, with whom they had struck an uneasy alliance.

Inspector Adams struggled once again.

Barton Jaeger, a chuckle bubbling up in his throat, brought the knife straight across the inspector's throat.

Once more, hot blood sprayed in Jaeger's face. This time as the sticky red blood splattered across his mouth, nose, and eyes, he smiled. He'd finally managed to get rid of the one man who'd threatened his whiskey-running empire.

He turned back to the cabin door, slipping from his wrist a Cree bracelet made of scrap metal and blue stones gathered from the nearby river.

He dropped it in the corner, where it would require a little effort to find. If he left it out in the open, the Mounties would know immediately it had been left behind to mislead them.

He opened the door, peeked out, and started his flight from the fort.

In the darkness, his wig of black braids, his buckskin shirt, and his dirty cotton pants marked him as an Indian. Just before he reached the gates, he let out a war whoop, knowing that somebody was bound to hear and most likely see him as well. He paused a few moments to give somebody the chance to get a good glimpse of him.

Then he ran fast to the horse he had waiting for him near the edge of the nearby river.

He felt a great joy. He had spent the past twelve years building a business on selling rot-gut whiskey and rifles to the Indians.

With Inspector Adams dead, Jaeger's business was going to be a lot better.

He reached his horse and rode off into the deep forest, lashing his animal with the reins, and smelling the sweet scent of the tall jack pines that surrounded him.

chapter
one

THE MOUNTIES HELD TO ONE BASIC BELIEF: THAT most problems could be resolved without physical force.

There were certain exceptions, and this morning was one of them.

Sitting in a chair in the interrogation room, which lay in the center of the guardhouse, was a singularly repellent man named Rivers. The kind of thug who made most Mounties forget all about their credo and want to punch the man's face in.

The three Mounties interrogating Rivers knew him well. He was, in no particular order, a thief, a rapist, an arsonist, and a sometimes gunny for the Barton Jaeger outfit. One lovely sonofabitch, to be sure.

This morning he was also one other contemptible thing: an informer.

Seems that last night Rivers had not only raped but severely beaten a young Indian woman who had been washing her clothes in the River Cree. Rivers had avoided jail before because either the women were too frightened to testify against him or because it was too dark to make any sort of positive identification. But last night's woman had not only recognized Rivers but was only too glad to tell the Mounties about it.

Rivers would be spending many well-deserved years behind bars in prison, which was why he was willing to give the men in the scarlet jackets some critical information in return for a "go easy" suggestion to the judge who tried him.

A tall, blond, handsome sergeant named Adams had a good idea of what Rivers was about to divulge and this was why the sergeant—who was after all the Mounties' most celebrated boxer—had a difficult time restraining himself. His instinct was to wade into the man, fists flying.

The inspector who had been murdered in his sleep last week had been Sergeant Adams's father.

"So how about it?" Rivers said. He was a runt whose checkered shirt and buckskin jacket and dungarees were filthy. Gnats and fleas buzzed around his hair and shoulders.

"How about what?" Adams said.

"A deal. I tell you who killed the inspector, you have the judge go easy on me at the trial."

Rivers, who was not exactly a scholar, had not yet made the connection between the Sergeant Adams leading the interrogation and the Inspector Adams who had been brutally slain last week. To him, the sergeant was just one more do-gooder Mountie got up in a scarlet Norfolk jacket, blue breeches with yellow stripes, and gleaming black boots.

"A Mountie died last week," Adams said, working hard at restraining himself.

Rivers shrugged. "Yeah, so I heard."

"If you had anything to do with it—" Adams's voice broke.

At this point, Sergeant Major Potts stepped into the bar of sunlight streaming through the barred windows. He looked sympathetically at Adams and said, "Why don't I question him for a while, Sergeant?"

Shaking, still wanting to smash in Rivers's face, Sergeant Adams saluted his superior officer, then went outside to light his pipe and try to relax.

Fort Cree was the hub of all civilization for this section of the Canada-Montana border. Within its walls, you found the same sights, sounds, and rhythms of any small town. The main buildings, all constructed of logs with sloped roofs, included barracks, officers' quarters, storehouses, stables, wagon sheds, and a parade grounds. Indians, half-breeds, and white men intermixed with the Mounties to trade, seek help, and complain constantly about what a bad job the scarlet coats were doing. A constable in the Royal Canadian Mounted Police earned seventy-five cents a day and for this he was expected to take undue amounts of guff and even risk his life on occasion. But there were pleasures, too, because the large majority of territory citizens were openly grateful for the work the Mounties did. Thanks to the men in the scarlet jackets, the Indian wars had largely been quelled, with the Indians for once actually getting a pretty good deal with the new treaties, and except for the ever-present whiskey runners, most of the outlaw gangs had been broken up. The Mounties had been founded in 1873 with fewer than three hundred men to patrol more than three hundred thousand square miles of raw Canadian wilderness. While making their appointed rounds they also performed the duties, when the need required, of doctor, nurse, social worker, tax collector, game warden, judge, and parson, too. One Mountie, many Yukon miles from any reinforcements, had joined with the people of a small village tired of being terrorized by bullies to set up his own police court. Stiff justice was meted out on the spot and the thugs soon left the villagers alone. Considering the odds against them, the Mounties had done a damn fine job.

And it didn't end there. The Mounties suffered not only external pressures but internal as well. Because it was difficult to remain a Mountie. While the men in scarlet coats came from many countries and many walks of life—in the barracks you heard proper English mixed with guttural English, and you heard a lot of French spoken as well—they all had to face one reality: If you weren't a good Mountie, then you didn't get to be a Mountie at all. Eager recruits were always waiting in line.

Sergeant Adams looked over at the barracks and thought of the life lived there. Hotheaded and sometimes angry men had to learn how to get along with each other. Fistfights were common and the occasional shooting incident could not be denied. Nor could the knife fights so popular among the French-speaking trappers. The barracks meant polishing boots, polishing the gold buttons on your coat, shaving, reading, talking, and watching the youngest and rawest recruits suffer from homesickness.

Sergeant Adams thought of all these things as he stood tamping his briar pipe in the sunny morning. The loss of his father was still acute. While the old man had never been demonstrative in his love for his sons, David Adams had always known that the old man loved him, especially after his mother died when the boys were in their early teen years. Then their rough-hewn father had fulfilled the role of mother, too.

There were many memories, too many really, but one of the most vivid was of the day David himself had become a Mountie. Before joining the Northwest Mounted Police, the old man had been a Dawson police officer, a job he'd been proud of to be sure, but the Mounties was another matter. To the old man the Mounties was the equivalent of a religious experience—the noblest calling on earth. David had seen the old man tear up exactly twice—on the day David's mother died, and on the day David donned the scarlet coat.

Adams glanced back at the guardhouse. In there sat a man who claimed to know who had killed David's father. Once he knew the answer, what would David do? The old man himself believed devoutly in the Mounties' creed of settling everything peacefully whenever possible. David knew he'd have to honor that credo if he was to honor the old man's memory.

He smoked his pipe, and watched Indian children play a game of tag on the soft green grass of the parade ground.

"You know this for a fact?"
"I heard it."
"From whom?"
"From one of his men."
"What was the name of this man?"
"Kinney."
"And he said what exactly?"
"I tole you."
"Tell me again."

"Jesus."

The interrogation had gotten intense about twenty minutes ago, just as David returned from smoking his pipe.

Sergeant Major Potts was one cold s.o.b. when he wanted to be, and apparently he wanted to be this morning. He fired question after unrelenting question at Rivers, never once trying to hide his contempt for the man.

Now, seeing that David was in control of himself again, Potts let Adams take over again.

He had one simple question.

"Who killed the inspector?"

"You put in a good word for me, you promise?"

"Answer the question."

Rivers looked frantically at Potts, as if he suspected their deal had been called off. "You put in a good word for me?"

Potts nodded. "I'll tell the judge that you cooperated in a capital case."

"You promise?"

"Answer the sergeant's question, Rivers," Potts said.

Rivers turned his attention back to David Adams. Rivers's teeth were little more than brown stubbs and when he sighed—even a few feet away—his breath made the Mounties grimace. Whoever drew this little bastard as a cell mate would probably end up hanging himself.

"It was Barton Jaeger," Rivers said.

So there it was. The Mounties neither moved nor spoke. All along there had been suspicion that Inspector Adams's death had only been rigged to look like a killing by an Indian, that it had actually been a white man responsible.

And now they knew.

Rivers wouldn't lie, not in this circumstance. To name Barton Jaeger as the killer seriously jeopardized Rivers's life. If he was going to try to deceive them, he'd certainly name somebody less powerful and vengeful than Jaeger.

"Some eyewitnesses say they saw an Indian running from the fort that night," Adams said. He kept saying over and over to himself that he was a Mountie and that he owed it to the memory of the old man to behave himself properly.

That was the only thing that kept him from grabbing Rivers and slapping his face bloody.

Rivers shook his head. "That was Jaeger. He wore an Indian getup and rubbed mink oil on his skin to make his face darker."

"You're sure the man who told you this wasn't lying?"

"No. He was laughing. Jaeger and his men think it's pretty funny. They think they got away with it."

Sergeant Major Potts looked over at David Adams. There was paternal sympathy in the older man's eyes. You didn't want to hear that the man who killed your father was laughing about it.

"Where's Jaeger now?" Adams said.

"In his stockade."

"The usual number of men?"

"From what I hear, he's added half a dozen or so."

"Why aren't you with him?"

Rivers shrugged. "We had a little falling out."

"About what?"

"What's it matter?"

"I asked you about what."

"Shit," Rivers said, and spat tobacco into a spittoon the men had placed at his feet. "What's the difference?" He looked sullenly up at Adams. Adams glared back at him. Rivers could see this was no man to irritate. He said, "I got drunk one night in the stockade and did something stupid."

"What was that?"

"Cheated at cards. One of the other boys thought it was his friend and shot him in the shoulder. Jaeger found out it was actually me cheatin' and blamed the whole thing on me."

No honor among thieves, Adams thought.

To Sergeant Major Potts, he said, "If you don't need me any longer, I'll excuse myself now, sir."

"Of course."

Adams saluted Potts, nodded good-bye to Potts's constable assistant, and then left the interrogation room without once looking at Rivers.

Couldn't take the chance. Might just start opening up on the little bastard and go against everything the Mounties believed in.

Half an hour later Sergeant Major Potts came into the barracks looking for the place where the men kept the punching bag they took turns using.

When he got there, he found a tall, muscular man stripped to his blue breeches with the yellow stripes and the gleaming black boots.

The man was muscular and quick. His taut body shone with sweat as he pounded the bag with a blinding series of punches, alternating hands and varying his attacks. The man's face was grim with anger, his eyes an icy blue, his prominent jaw set hard.

The man was, of course, David Adams.

Potts had accompanied David on his first snow patrol. Potts—at the request of David's father—had given David several days' instruction on how to snowshoe and then Potts had led a six-day expedition into snow country, setting out in horse-drawn bobsleighs and trailing two dog teams that hauled tents, blankets, and food on their toboggans. It had been quite a trip. After leaving the bobsleigh, they'd trekked even deeper into the wilderness and captured six whiskey runners, bringing back all of them alive to stand trial. Potts had known right from the start that David Adams was an exceptional Mountie.

"Sorry it was so rough in there," Sergeant Major Potts said.

At first, Adams seemed not to hear him. He just kept pounding the leather bag.

"Maybe I shouldn't have called you in for the interrogation at all," Potts went on. "Maybe it wasn't the right thing at all."

Finally, Adams seemed to hear the other man. He turned his icy gaze on him, even though his punches kept coming with powerful regularity.

"You know what I want to do, don't you, sir?"

"Yes, son, I do."

"And I hope you're planning to let me do it."

"Do you think you can handle it?"

"Yessir."

"That you can remember that you're a Mountie and conduct yourself accordingly?"

"Yessir."

"I can't spare more than seven men."

"Seven men will do fine, sir, in addition to Frank and myself."

"Those are great odds. Jaeger will probably have thirty or more at the stockade."

"I'm not afraid, sir."

And with that, Adams returned his attention to the punching bag. The punches came even faster now. The bag was slammed so hard, it threatened to tear from its mooring. Adams's back and shoulders rippled with muscles.

Sergeant Major Potts stood staring at the young man. Poor kid. Inspector Adams, while gruff, had been a caring father and a real loss both to David and the Mounties. Barton Jaeger had to be held accountable for his actions, and despite some of Potts's reservations, he knew that David was the man to lead the search party into the hills to the west where Barton Jaeger ran a virtual fiefdom.

He took one last glance at David, at the fury in the punches, and decided that no matter how many men Jaeger had, David Adams was going to give him a real fight.

Sergeant Major Potts left the barracks and went to round up the six men who would accompany David Adams tomorrow at dawn.

chapter
two

LATER THAT SAME AFTERNOON, A MAN CAME
riding along the trail to Fort Cree. His mount was a
calico. His sheepskin jacket, worn out of deference to
the suddenly cooling day, bore a badge that identified
him as a U.S. Marshal. Given the frequent cooperation
between the Mounties and American law enforcement
officials, it was a badge seen often in this part of Canada.

In the warm sunlight, the fort was a welcome sight to Frank
Adams. He'd been four days on the trail from Bozeman
where he'd been testifying against a killer in federal court,
and he had been summoned on the worst kind of mission.
His younger brother David had wired him that their father
had been murdered.

This made it an especially hard year for Frank. In Feb-
ruary, Sarah, his wife of sixteen years, had died of whooping cough. Their only child, a boy, had died two years
earlier of influenza. All this showed on the hard face of
Frank Adams. Unlike his brother, he was neither tall nor
handsome, but short, given to extra weight, and likewise
given to long periods of grieving.

In the strong light, Frank saw the Cree wigwams that
were arranged outside the fort itself. Smoke came from
some of the wigwams, and big and little children ran merrily
about while mothers prepared the evening meal. Several
elder Cree sat around a fire in the center of the wigwams
smoking pipes and talking. They paid him little interest.

Inside the fort, Frank went straight to the stable. His horse
needed food and water and a place to bed down for the night.

13

He started walking toward the mess hall, where he assumed he would find his brother at this time, but on his way he passed by several straw shooting targets set up against the back of the fort. Here was where all the young recruits developed their shooting skills.

Frank, a marksman himself, had a difficult time resisting the targets.

He fast-drew his Colt .45 from his holster and let fly.

The bullets barked on the sunny, late afternoon air.

Frank was aware, by now, that he had a small audience. Three raw-looking youths who were obviously recruits stood watching him with a mixture of awe and fear.

One of the youngsters ran up to the target, examined the surface, and called back, "He hit four bull's-eyes!"

"Nobody's ever done that at this fort, not with six shots," one of the other recruits said. He stood close to Frank and grinned at him. "Who are you, mister?"

"Name's Adams."

The two recruits glanced at each other. "Adams?"

Frank nodded grimly. "Inspector Adams was my father. David is my brother."

From down by the target, the third recruit shouted, "You got two guns. You want to try the other one?"

Frank grinned. "You boys must be starved for entertainment."

"Just never seen nobody shoot like you before, mister."

The third recruit ran halfway back to his friends and then stood off to the side so Frank could shoot.

This time he shot six bull's-eyes.

"If you boys don't mind, I think I'll get me some food. I'm kind of hungry." Frank holstered his six-shooter and turned to the front of the fort. "Say, by the way, you think I could wash up in the barracks before I head for the mess hall?"

"Mister," one of the recruits said breathlessly, "we'd consider it an honor if you wash up in the same place we do."

By the time Frank finished cleaning up, word about his prowess with a six-shooter was racing around the mess.

When he ducked inside the building where everybody was eating, two of the recruits who'd watched him shoot pointed to him.

A hush fell over the mess. It was as if Wild Bill Hickok and Jesse James had just walked in the door together.

Frank found David near the back, sitting with two other Mounties at a long table. The meal was the same as virtually every other night, buffalo patties, pork and beans, flapjacks and tea.

Despite the solemn occasion—two brothers coming together after the murder of their father—David had heard the buzz about his brother's shooting prowess and said, "It's the fastest gun in the West." He grinned at his brother and clapped him on the back.

"Word gets around fast on this post." Frank grinned back.

"Well, you've got to remember that a lot of these boys are straight off the farm and they don't often get to see shooting like that." Then he got serious. "If we had the time, I wouldn't mind you giving them some pointers on how to handle their Enfield revolvers. The boys aren't always the best shots."

Frank laughed. "You're still tryin' to get me into the Mounties, aren't you?"

"Not a bad idea, brother. Not a bad idea at all."

Then he indicated a place for both of them at the table and they sat down.

David made introductions. The other two non-coms stayed a few minutes, making conversation and telling Frank how sorry they were about his father, and then they said that they were headed back to the other part of the barracks, where night life often consisted of mending clothes, writing letters home, and reading the latest novels that were being passed around.

After they left, David said, "Damn, it's good to see you, brother."

Frank nodded. With his squat body and dark hair, he looked little like an Adams. His green eyes completed the difference. "Any leads other than the Indian one?"

David nodded. "Thanks to a slimy little bastard named Rivers, I think we've got our man." He leaned forward, his red coat still bright in the lamplit dusk. "Barton Jaeger."

Frank's face said nothing. He received the news in his usual quiet way. He knew who Jaeger was, of course. Jaeger often ran forays into Montana.

"I'm going after him," David said.

"When?"

"Tomorrow morning."

"I'm going with you."

For the first time since his father's death, David smiled. "I was hoping you'd say that. This is something we should share."

Frank leaned forward. For all his quietness, he was an intense man, and he'd never looked more intense than he did right now. "I don't plan to bring him back alive, brother."

"I guess we'll just have to see what happens."

"As long as we understand each other, David."

"I can't condone cold-blooded murder, Frank. I'm a Mountie. You know the code. Our father lived by it."

"If I get any chance at all, I'll kill him. I just want you to know that."

And with that, knowing that he was working them both into too much of a stir, Frank leaned back, took out his makings, and rolled himself a cigarette.

For the next twenty minutes, Frank drank coffee and smoked cigarettes, and watched the barracks clean out as men drifted to various duties and pastimes before lights out at 10:15.

David smoked his pipe and drank coffee. They talked about the funeral service the Mounties had given their father, and about the way various of their relatives had received the news, and then they talked about the terrible years Frank had had lately, what with his boy and his wife dying.

Afterward, they went for a walk around the fort. This lightened the mood. Though Frank had been here before, he'd never spent much time learning about daily life, and it genuinely seemed to interest him, especially the games the men played, notably rugby football, tug-of-war, and cricket, all of which became hazardous because of all the gopher holes in the ground.

David introduced Frank to a young man who was the day's room orderly—and the young man didn't exactly look happy. Men took turns being room orderly for their particular barracks. It wasn't a fun job. You spent the day making sure everything was spic and span, including the mess kits that the room orderly had to wash out, and then he had to go to the quartermaster to get the day's ration of bread for his group of men. Bread was given out only sparingly at the fort each day.

When they were finished touring the facilities, David showed Frank where he could bunk down for the night. The men said good night and Frank went to his small room. He didn't bother lighting the kerosene lamp. He stripped down to his long johns and got beneath the covers.

As always, suspicious lawman that he was, he lay on his back, keeping his fingers on his Colt in case he needed it quickly.

He went to sleep quickly. He needed rest. He had been many days on the trail. He wanted to be fresh when he met the man who'd murdered his father.

Recruit James Carmichael was born to raise hell.

This was what he'd had tattooed on his right forearm anyway, one night when whiskey made the twenty-three-year-old more foolish than usual.

Like many other farmers, sailors, lumberjacks, and day laborers, Carmichael had joined the Mounties for adventure. He dreamt of great, vast Indian wars, and barn dances where you met local beauties, and of himself handsome and impressive in a scarlet coat.

Well, he'd gotten the scarlet coat all right but what went with it was not untold adventure but instead a mundane series of duties around the fort. For the first year of his enlistment, Carmichael found himself a teamster, wood chopper, whip sawyer, mortar bearer, clay hauler, and roof plasterer. He wasn't singled out for these duties—many other recruits who'd also dreamed of great adventures worked right alongside him.

But Carmichael was different. He took these tasks as a personal affront to his manhood.

Which was why, when he first got the chance six months ago, he became a spy for the Barton Jaeger outfit.

Just as Frank Adams was falling asleep, Carmichael, dressed in a dark sweater and dark trousers, waited for the sentry to walk to the other end of the fort, and then snuck out of the gate and into the darkness.

The Cree who camped along the river were mostly asleep now, too, their central fire guttering, their wigwams silent.

The night was chilly and smelled of dew and woodsmoke. The moon was only a quarter but bright.

In a copse of birches by the flowing water, a half-breed with the unlikely named of Prine stepped from the shadows and greeted Carmichael with a raised hand. Prine was a runner for the Barton Jaeger outfit.

"Evening, Harry," Carmichael said, a certain irony in his tone. He found it endlessly amusing that a breed would have a white man's name, proof to Carmichael that nobody really wanted to be an Indian.

"There is news?" Prine said. He was a tall, muscular man whose good looks were ruined by his constant scowl. He wore his black hair long. Jammed in his belt was a knife that looked capable of cutting a log in half and an old black powder pistol that the breed took great pride in showing off.

"Big news," Carmichael said.

And proceeded to tell Prine about Rivers's fingering Barton Jaeger as the killer, and about the arresting party that would tomorrow leave for Barton Jaeger's stockade, and the arrival of David Adams's brother, Frank. "He's a mean-looking bastard. Tell Jaeger he looks like he could be rough."

"There will be nine in all, then?"

"Yes."

"And they leave at dawn?"

"Those are the plans."

Prine nodded.

No matter how much money Jaeger paid him, and Jaeger paid him quite well actually, there was a small part of Carmichael that didn't feel quite right about being a spy. It didn't square with his rugged he-man image of himself. He got like this especially when the talk turned to Jaeger hurting one of the other Mounties. While Carmichael didn't have much love for the scarlet coats as an institution—why did they have to settle all the goddamn Indian wars before he signed on?—he did like many of his coworkers as individuals.

The breed smiled. "The Mounties will be easy to find in their scarlet coats."

Carmichael didn't smile along. Instead he looked down at the river that now smelled of fish. Moonlight lay a silver patina over the clay banks and the rushing water.

Prine surveyed the fort in the distance. "Have they chosen the men who are going in the party?"

"Yes. This afternoon."

"You are not among them?"

"No." Thank God, Carmichael wanted to say. If his friends were bushwacked by Jaeger's men, he certainly didn't want to be there to see it.

The breed nodded to his mount that he'd ground-tied on the other side of the trees. "I need to get back now."

"Yes. You'd better hurry."

Prine wasn't big on formal good-byes. He simply turned around and walked away. No good-bye of any sort. He simply vanished into the shadows.

Soon enough there was the sound of unshod hooves against the soft spring earth. He splashed across the river, which was relatively shallow at this point, and then appeared on the bank across the way. For a moment, in moonlit silhouette, he almost looked like a statue of the noble red man. But then Carmichael remembered the man's constant silent rage and reconsidered the "noble" part.

• • •

The moment he got back to the barracks, Carmichael knew something was wrong. All the men were outside, forming a ring around somebody.

Carmichael pushed his way in for a peek.

Lying on the ground was a recruit named R. J. Grieves. He was shirtless and sockless. He wore only his breeches. Even from here, Carmichael could see that the man was sleek with sweat. His chest and stomach heaved greatly. Somewhere close by, Carmichael could smell vomit.

The man kneeling next to him was a brawling, red-haired recruit named Joey Hanrahan or "Doc" as he was known. While not a real doctor, Hanrahan spent a lot of his free time in the barracks reading medical books. He actually seemed to know what he was talking about, so much so that many of the men went to him now with all their aches and pains. Like many Mounties, he had come from a family that was poor but obstinate about improving its lot. Joey Hanrahan might not have the legal paper pronouncing him a doctor but he was certainly in the process of accumulating the knowledge.

Now, putting a hand to R. J. Grieves's forehead, Hanrahan said, "When are you boys going to listen to me? You're like a bunch of little kids. I told you not to eat any kind of berries you didn't recognize, didn't I? Look at Grieves here. He's got it comin' out of both ends."

And as if to confirm Hanrahan's judgment, Grieves just then jerked upward. It was clear almost at once that he'd fouled himself. The stench was sickening sweet.

"Is he gonna die?" one of the young constables asked.

"No, he ain't gonna die," Hanrahan said. "He's just gonna wish he did."

Carmichael had had enough.

He wanted shadow and sleep now. He'd earned his Judas money and was feeling less than proud of himself.

He was ten steps from the barracks door when he saw Sergeant Major Potts, in full uniform including the brass-spiked white helmet he'd taken to wearing since taking charge of the fort following the death of Inspector Adams.

"Carmichael?"

"Yes, sir."

"You saw how sick Grieves is."

"Yes, sir."

"That means he won't be able to go on patrol with Sergeant Adams."

"Yes, sir."

"I need a man to take his place."

"But, sir, I—"

He couldn't believe it. Go on the same patrol he'd just told Barton Jaeger about?

"You have some objection to that?"

Carmichael knew better than to piss off Sergeant Major Potts. Even before the death of his friend Adams, he'd been known as one hot-tempered officer.

"No, sir. No objection."

"Good. Be ready to leave at dawn, then."

"Yessir."

Carmichael saluted and staggered into the barracks. He still couldn't believe what he'd just been ordered to do. Just couldn't believe it at all.

chapter
three

PRINE REACHED JAEGER'S STOCKADE JUST AFTER
daylight. The two men posted to the north made a big
thing of waving him through with their rifles. The men in
the camp took every opportunity to remind him that he was a
breed and therefore subject to the white man's authority.

He came in on a big bay mare that showed the effects
of a hard, relentless run.

As always, the stockade looked and smelled of filth. Col-
lected here were the scum of Canada—ex-convicts, killers,
kidnappers, thieves of every description—and they lived
accordingly in tents, lean-tos, half-ass cabins long in need
of cleaning.

Only Barton Jaeger himself had a decent abode, a house
of logs with a hinged door, glass windows, and, lately, lace
curtains. Everybody knew who'd put the curtains there—
the married woman from the nearby settlement Jaeger snuck
off to see most nights. The woman had been here only once
but she'd taken the time to fix up Jaeger's cabin.

Dogs nipped at the mare as Prine finished his ride through
camp. Nowhere, not even on the scruffy faces of the children,
did he see a smile. Prine was a man alone in the stockade, a
legendary tracker who could smell water at five miles and
follow track even at night, but a man nobody white liked
or trusted. He made his hatred of white people too plain.

Outside Jaeger's cabin, he dismounted and went up to the
door. He knocked once and went inside without waiting.

The beefy but sleek dark-haired man sitting behind the
long table facing the door didn't look as if he belonged

23

in a stockade like this one. He wore a black string tie, a white shirt with ruffles, and a large ruby ring. A stranger might call him a fop but he would soon be a dead stranger because the man's dark eyes told the whole story. Barton Jaeger, for all his slick city ways, was a man given to quick and remorseless violence. Jaeger was one of a special breed in the Canadian wilderness, men who came to this wild land to amass a fortune and then head back to gentler climes. Jaeger had gone to Europe three times in the past few years where it was rumored he'd already put a great deal of money away.

"Next time you come in without knocking, breed, you're going to get that red ass of yours shot off," Jaeger said, looking up from his perpetual game of solitaire.

"There is news," Prine said, disregarding Jaeger's irritation. Jaeger was always threatening Prine but he needed the breed too much to ever really do anything. Jaeger was anything but stupid. Prine was worth any six white men, and good white men at that.

"Oh? Such as what?"

"Inspector Adams's two sons are headed here along with a patrol from Fort Cree."

Jaeger said, "So Frank Adams came up here, too, did he?"

"You know this Frank?" Prine asked. Jaeger sounded as if he were holding back a secret.

"Oh, yes, I know him." Jaeger smiled.

Prine didn't return Jaeger's smile. "You kill a man's father, you should be afraid of that man, no matter who he is."

Jaeger laughed. "More Cree wisdom? You're just full of that kind of thing, aren't you, Prine?" He smirked. "And you're full of shit, too."

As usual, Prine ignored the insult. His time to pay Jaeger back for all the slights and innuendos would come soon enough. In the meantime, he would simply abide Jaeger and tolerate his nonsense.

Prine glanced around the cabin. The Weller woman had done a pleasant job with the interior. In addition to the lace curtains, she'd also laid down hook rugs and put sheets and a comforter on the bed. She'd placed spittoons and ashtrays throughout the cabin as well, giving the cabin one more thing it had never had—cleanliness.

Much as he pretended to hate all this womanly fuss, Jaeger actually liked it. He saw it as proof positive that Louise—for all her confusion about their relationship—actually did love him, and that they had a future together. His plan was to run away with her to Europe—and soon.

All he had to figure out was what to do about that husband of hers who spent all day in a wheelchair ever since a tree had fallen over on him during a logging accident and crushed his legs.

Prine thought about all these things as he turned his attention back to Jaeger. He knew these things about the white man because Jaeger, for all his pretended sophistication, was so transparent—a vain and bullying man who was now deeply in love with somebody else's wife.

"How many men are they bringing?" Jaeger said.

"Seven, with themselves."

"And they're how far away?"

"Another day."

Jaeger leaned back in his chair and picked up a cigar. He bit off the end with a certain ritualistic violence, spat the end in a wastebasket, and put the stogie in his teeth. "It wasn't just the old man Adams I hated."

"Meaning?"

"Meaning two years ago, Frank Adams sent my brother to prison."

Jaeger thought of his brother, a fool and an incompetent, but his brother nonetheless. Carl had gotten drunk before the robbery of a Montana bank and had panicked when the bank president had called for help. Instead of grabbing the money and running, Jaeger's brother Carl had opened fire, bringing the law double-quick. He hadn't lasted long, surrendering within half an hour. From there, after a quick trial, he'd gone to prison. Because Marshal Adams had been the arresting officer, Jaeger had always held him responsible for his brother's fate.

"I want you to take Frank Adams."

"What?"

"Grab him at night. Bring him back here."

"But why? We can handle the patrol."

Jaeger stared at him. "If anybody should understand hate, breed, it's you. You know how you hate us whites? Well, that's how I hate the Adamses. Every time I'm enjoying myself, I get interrupted by this thought of my brother. In prison. What he's going through. It isn't fun, believe me. And he's got eight more goddamn years to go. Does that tell you anything about why I want you to bring Frank Adams here?"

Prine nodded. There was no use arguing with Jaeger when he was like this. He was a man of big emotions—lust, greed, and most especially vengeance. Nobody was ever foolish enough to cross Jaeger, not even Prine himself.

"I'll leave in an hour and pick up their trail." Prine nodded and started to leave.

Jaeger stopped him. "There's one more thing, breed."

Prine stared at the front door, eager to be gone. He knew what Jaeger was about to say.

"The Fallon woman," Jaeger said.

Prine tensed.

"Some of the men, the white men, seem to be think there's something going on between you two. Personally, I don't give a shit what you do. You can screw turkeys for all I care. But you know how these people are about Indians and whites mixing. I can't afford to have my little village here disrupted. You understand me, breed?"

"I understand."

"Good. Then I don't want to hear any more about it."

Prine opened the door and went outside.

A pair of dark blue eyes watched Prine leave Jaeger's cabin.

The eyes returned swiftly to the cabin door, watching, waiting.

Brother Edmund—real name Harold Carlson—was originally from Buffalo, New York. He had initially come to

Oregon fifteen years ago bringing a wife and two children, all of whom had died in the process. Their deaths had changed Carlson. Though he'd never been a religious man before, he now professed to hear God directly and personally, the Creator telling Harold—who by this time was known, somewhat sarcastically, as Brother Edmund—all the things he expected the man to do on this earth.

Eventually, as did many disillusioned travelers, Carlson moved up the map to Canada, which seemed to hold even more promise than America—gold and timber and outlaw empires that were as powerful as the armies of certain small nations. He also remarried and started a new family.

Ultimately, Brother Edmund wound up here, at Jaeger's stockade, because he hated the Mounties so much. The men in red had too often chased religious tribes away—especially when the tribes got into hassles with the settlers who tilled the land and felled the trees. Settlers mostly saw Brother Edmund and his kind as a nuisance. Brother Edmund in turn saw most "law-abiding" people as vermin. In this way, he justified what the people of the stockade did. If they lied, cheated, brutalized, and murdered people, that was all right with Brother Edmund because their victims were all friends of the Mounties.

But now Brother Edmund had a problem with one of the people of the stockade—with Jaeger himself. The day Louise Weller had come here to visit Jaeger, Brother Edmund's two-year-old girl had died of a sudden and violent fever. Brother Edmund knew exactly what had happened of course. While the Lord might abide the other things the stockade people did, He would never tolerate such a sin of the flesh as adultery.

The Weller woman—clearly a harlot—had killed his daughter as certainly as if she'd plunged a knife into the infant's frail chest. She should not have come here to see Jaeger. The Lord punished Brother Edmund's daughter for this. The Lord worked in mysterious ways and you never knew what He was going to be up to next.

And now as Brother Edmund watched Jaeger step out on his porch to smoke a cigar, he promised himself that someday soon he would see the Weller woman again and carry out God's will.

For now, Brother Edmund went about his work but most of the time he thought about Jaeger and the harlot and the destruction their sinfulness had wrought on his family.

Prine kept a wigwam down by the creek. He went there now, spending the first fifteen minutes splashing around in the chill silver water and getting himself clean, and then standing in the wigwam and putting on fresh clothes.

He was just pulling on his leggings when he heard the familiar bird call. He had taught her how to press her lips together and make the sound.

He went over to the flap and threw it back.

Anne Fallon stood outside the wigwam, more heartbreakingly beautiful than ever.

Shy as ever, too. "I thought I saw you ride in."

For the first few moments he just stared at her. The feelings she evoked in him were both wonderful and terrible—wonderful because he loved her so much, terrible because, as a breed, there was nothing he could do about his feelings. Jaeger was right. Every white man anyplace they'd go would do everything he could to pull the two apart.

Prine nodded to the stockade. "They'll see you."

"I don't care."

Prine sighed. "Jaeger had another talk with me about you."

Anger showed in her brown eyes. "And I especially don't care what Jaeger thinks."

Rather than invite her in, he came outside, letting the flap fall behind him.

In the afternoon light, her long auburn hair sparkling, she looked more beautiful than ever. Even her faded gingham dress, washed too many times in the creek and then pounded against granite rock, seemed regal on her slender but womanly body.

She was nineteen. Her father hated Indians and especially hated the arrogant Prine. Yellow fever had taken her mother. She loved Prine and saw what his love for her had done to him—made him care about somebody who was white.

He looked at her now. Pain was evident on his handsome face. "I've been thinking."

"You want to end it, don't you?"

"It would be better."

"For who? Jaeger? For the scum in this stockade?"

"For both of us."

She was a few inches shorter than Prine. Now, staring up at him, she squinted into the sunlight. "I've never thought of you as a coward, Prine."

Prine looked across the long grass separating his wigwam from the stockade proper. A couple of the outlaws' wives had gathered by a clothesline, long johns and towels flapping in the breeze, and were looking at them and whispering.

Always, the whispering.

"We have an audience," Prine said.

"I don't care."

He wanted to take her in his arms, hold her. He had never even kissed her. He was afraid.

"You take care of Lona," he said. Lona was her young sister. "That will give you plenty to do."

"Damn you, Prine!" she said.

And this time, he did not have to hint that she should go away. She turned and stormed off, headed back toward the stockade and the leering eyes of the gossipy wives.

She favored them with a burning look, one they gladly returned. Like most folks, they did not cotton to women who gave themselves, in any sense, to Indians, even half-breeds.

Prine went back into his wigwam.

Except for some buffalo robes, a few books he'd learned to read at missionary school, and the clothes he'd bought a few years ago at the settlement store, the wigwam was empty.

He went over and picked up his carbine. Hefted it. At least Jaeger had given him an interesting assignment. He would track the Adams patrol until he found some way to overpower and kidnap Frank Adams.

At least life held a few agreeable tasks, anyway.

When he left the wigwam, he paused momentarily and glanced across at the stockade. Anne Fallon's cabin lay near the slope of a grassy hill. He could see her now in the yard, sawing logs to heat her place. Slender she might be but she was in no way weak.

A familiar pain announced itself in Prine's chest. He knew he would never love another woman the way he loved Anne. But he also knew that their feelings for each other were hopeless. That was why he'd never touched her. He wanted her to have a good life and not be "soiled" when she finally gave herself to the white man she took as her husband.

Thinking all this, he walked over to the corral, looked over the available stock, and chose a roan for his ride out this late morning.

Ten minutes later he was guiding his horse up into the piney hills surrounding the stockade.

He was on his way to kidnap Frank Adams. While David Adams had every intention of coming here anyway, knowing that his brother was being held captive might make him behave stupidly.

Barton Jaeger stood on the stoop of his cabin, watching Prine ride away. Soon enough now, he would repay the Adams family in yet another way: He would get his hands on Frank Adams and be able to lure David Adams into the stockade.

Jaeger's thoughts were interrupted by sudden shouting from the other end of the encampment.

Children, women, and barnyard animals all ran toward the commotion, so Jaeger joined in.

Down by the creek, framed against a copse of pine trees, two huge men were brawling.

One was a white man named Dubois and the other a Mexican named Hernendez. Dubois was generally considered the toughest man in the encampment.

Right now, they were fighting fair, with fists and feet only, though this would change soon enough.

As the boss of the stockade, Jaeger had a right to stop them, to tell them to save their strength for the battles with the Mounties, but he knew that the whole stockade enjoyed a good bloody battle and so he let it go on.

Both men were bare-chested, both heavily covered with hair.

Dubois stood upright, keeping his fists up in the way of a professional boxer. Hernendez was a street-fighter, lashing out with fists and feet whenever he got the chance.

Dubois hit Hernendez a smashing blow to the forehead. It staggered the Mexican, who went wobbling back several feet. Blood started oozing from the Mexican's nose.

But Hernendez was hardly out of the fight.

From nowhere came his left foot, catching Dubois in the groin.

Dubois was the one who wobbled now, shouting out a string of curses and holding his crotch tenderly.

But he was also playing possum. Seeing how much he'd hurt his opponent, Hernendez came in closer than he should have—and Dubois's left, then right fist crashed into the Mexican's face.

The crowd cheered as Dubois began alternating his punches, left, right, left, right, with Hernendez unable to defend himself in any way.

But Hernendez was tough.

Shaky as his legs were, he had the composure to draw his knife, a big, ugly variation on a Bowie knife, with dried blood staining the plain wooden hilt.

He flashed it in front of both Dubois and the crowd. Both seemed suitably impressed.

A man from the crowd yelled at Dubois and then tossed the big man a knife for his own use.

Just as Hernendez had done, Dubois showed the knife off to both the crowd and his opponent.

Another cheer came up from the onlookers, and a few of the little kids began applauding.

There was now a good chance that one of these men would be killed and that always made for the best kind of fight possible.

The two men started circling each other in wide circles. Both cursed; both spat.

Hernendez struck the first blow.

He came in under the arc Dubois was cutting with his knife and slashed a deep cut clean across Dubois's chest.

The man's matted black chest hair glistened now with his own blood.

The crowd was duly appreciative, oohing and aahing and reassessing Hernendez. Maybe he could beat Dubois, after all.

But for all the blood that was pouring from his chest, Dubois seemed unfazed.

He now started coming straight at Hernendez.

This clearly made the Mexican nervous.

His dark eyes began flashing around furtively as if he were looking for some place to run.

But it was Hernendez who got the second cut in as well.

Dubois had feinted left as he prepared to cut the Mexican but then Dubois clumsily tripped over a rock and started to pitch forward.

Hernendez was quick enough to lean forward and slash his knife across Dubois's shoulder.

Dubois's cry was enough to shake the entire stockade.

Clearly, the man had been hurt.

But then Hernendez made his first mistake.

Not understanding that men like Dubois are most dangerous when they've been hurt, Hernendez decided to move in fast for the kill.

He took three steps forward.

Dubois was still hunched over in pain, blood now soaking his entire torso, his shoulder wound pumping more and more of the red stuff every moment.

To the untutored eye, Dubois had never looked more vulnerable.

But then Hernendez, obviously thinking that Dubois was incapacitated now, leaned in to stab Dubois in the neck.

Dubois came up from his crouch like a black bear who has been suppressing rage for too long.

The first thing that Dubois did was throw his own knife away.

The second thing Dubois did was grab Hernendez's knife arm and break his wrist.

The snapping sound could be heard throughout the stockade.

The third thing Dubois did was kick Hernendez in the stomach.

And then Dubois got serious.

He waded into the other man delivering rights and lefts of such amazing speed and power that most people couldn't even see them.

He broke his nose, then his jaw, then he crushed the ridge of bone above Hernendez's left eye.

He returned the crotch kick that the Mexican had earlier delivered to him, kicking him so hard in the groin that the Mexican was lifted up off his feet.

Then Dubois went back to punching.

He would not let the Mexican fall down.

And suddenly the crowd realized what they were seeing here.

Dubois was going to beat the Mexican to death before their very eyes.

Which was what he did.

It took him five more minutes. He used both his fists and his feet. He constantly had to hold Hernendez up so he could hit him. A few times the Mexican managed to squeak out little pleas for mercy but he had enraged Dubois and so there was no mercy at all left in the white man.

He pounded away.

As he watched all this, knowing what was about to happen, Jaeger wondered again if he should step in.

But then he started watching the faces of the people, adults and children alike, at the slightly glazed eyes, at the drool in the corners of their mouths, at the excited way their hands clapped together.

They would talk about this event for years afterward and in some perverse way, it would make them proud of living in the stockade.

And they would hate him forever—rebel against him, too, at some future date—if he tried to stop it.

So he lighted a cigar and watched the rest of the battle.

Dubois came in close again, hitting the Mexican hard in the stomach, then clubbing him on the side of the head with a fast right hand.

And then not even Dubois could hold him up anymore.

The Mexican fell over backward, dust rising as his body slammed into the ground.

There was no doubt he was dead. No doubt at all.

At first, there was a hushed silence as the onlookers exchanged glances and then looked at the corpse on the ground. It was almost as if they didn't know how to act.

But then one woman broke the silence. She whipped off her gingham bonnet and threw it high in the air and yelled "Yippee!"

And then everybody joined in.

It was like a barn dance and a birthday celebration and Christmas all rolled into one.

People jumped up and down and shouted and some of the children formed a ring around the grizzled, bloody form of Dubois and began dancing around the man who offered them a big, bloody grin.

Jaeger just let them go.

People had to have their fun and if the cost of that fun was occasionally the life of a Mexican, then so be it.

The people started to wave for Jaeger to come down and join the party—a jug of corn liquor had now made its inevitable appearance—and so Jaeger went to have himself a little fun.

chapter
four

A FEW HOURS BEFORE PRINE REACHED JAEGER'S stockade, Sergeant David Adams led his patrol from Fort Cree.

David had spent extra time getting the proper horses. From the beginning, the Mounties had had a tradition of obtaining only the best horses, and the right mount for each man. The commissioner at Regina headquarters believed that one of a man's biggest assets was a horse he could trust to get him through, a horse he personally groomed, fed, and befriended. This tradition was carried out whenever possible.

A constable named McKenzie rode on one side of David Adams while Frank Adams rode on the other. The officers at Fort Cree had decided that McKenzie was a good bet for being officer material so it was decided to give him every chance at leadership.

This patrol was bound to prove useful to a man moving up as quickly as McKenzie.

The men rode on.

Jaeger sat on the edge of his bed, rubbing sleep from his face and trying to reconstruct the nightmare.

The dark images of the dream lingered: Louise Weller was on a train pulling out of the station. He ran and ran to catch it but he could never quite reach the last car. Finally, the train vanished into the distance, the entire earth filled suddenly with the sound of Louise's laughter. Jaeger felt like an orphan, abandoned and alone in a dark, frightening

world where shadows hid unspeakable terrors. Memories
of his own boyhood in a London orphanage then began to
flood his mind and he came awake.

"Jaeger?"

"Yes."

"It's Brother Edmund."

The man stood outside the cabin door. Jaeger didn't want
to start the day by listening to his craziness.

"Come back later."

"I just wanted to see if you wanted some elderberry wine
my wife made."

"Go away."

"The Lord be with you."

"Yeah," Jaeger said, rising from his bed, the nightmare
still clinging to him like morning fog. "Yeah, I'm sure
He is."

He went over and washed his face in the basin and thought:
I've got to see Louise soon.

Soon.

By the time Constable Abernathy saw the snake, it was
too late. Abernathy's mount had already been struck and
was now rearing up, pitching the lean, angular Mountie off
its back, sending him crashing into a boulder lying by the
side of the dusty trail.

Abernathy's flat pillbox hat flew off, despite the chin
strap, as the back of his head struck the boulder.

He was unconscious instantly.

He came awake thinking he'd been discovered. Somehow his friends in the Mounties had learned who he really was.

Far more painful than his thumping headache was the
possibility that he'd been uncovered at last.

"Can you see me all right?"

The man leaning in and speaking was Sergeant David
Adams, leader of the patrol.

"Yessir," Abernathy said.

"Does your head hurt?"

"Yessir."

"Are you dizzy?"

"Not too bad, I guess."

"Was it a snake?"

"Yessir."

Sergeant Adams looked up at his brother Frank and said, "Want to give me a hand?"

The two men leaned in and carefully helped Abernathy to his feet.

Just then, beyond a copse of trees, there was the echo of a loud gunshot, and then a quick sad animal sound.

They'd had to put the horse down.

"Poor guy," Abernathy said. He'd loved horses since he was a boy. Shooting them was about the worst thing he could imagine, even when it was necessary.

Sergeant Adams was leaning in again, checking Abernathy's eyes for any evidence of concussion. Apparently he saw none because he leaned back and said, "Why don't you try walking."

"Yessir."

He went twenty feet down the trail, then turned around and came back.

Several other constables stood around watching him. They weren't unhappy about this pause in riding. Backs and buttocks got sore.

Abernathy came back to the Adams brothers.

"Should I take the extra horse, sir?"

Sergeant Adams nodded. "You want to sit down for a while?"

"I'm fine, sir." It was important to Constable Abernathy not to sound like a whiner.

"You're sure?"

"I'm sure."

Sergeant Adams smiled, obviously pleased with the spunk the young man showed.

"All right, then," he said, "let's resume riding."

Beautiful as it was, this was treacherous terrain for men riding horses. Buttes and bluffs and coulees and tawny plains concealed rocky ground that hooves often tripped over.

Plus there was the even greater enemy of boredom. Even after a single day riding, men on patrol began to pay less attention to their surroundings, and thus leave themselves open to all kinds of attack. Only the sight of big-game animals drew their attention, the moose and elk and white-tailed deer and black bears that roamed the heavily forested hills and mountains.

It had been four hours since Constable Abernathy's unfortunate spill and Sergeant David Adams was thinking about taking one more break before pushing on into nightfall.

Next to him, his brother Frank said, "He knows we're coming."

"Jaeger?"

Frank nodded.

"I suppose he does."

Frank let the reins draw easy in his gloved hands as the patrol moved along the trail. "Probably somebody up in those hills trailing us."

David glanced over at his brother and smiled. "You thinking of going up there and smoking him out?"

Frank smiled back. "Guess I have to admit the notion did cross my mind."

"You getting bored?"

"A little I suppose."

David laughed. "You miss the gunplay. I was reading an article in one of our magazines that said a U.S. lawman uses his gun more in one month than an average Mountie uses his in five years."

"You bragging or complaining, brother?"

"Neither. Just stating a fact." This time, David kept his smile to himself. He didn't want to make Frank think that he, as a Mountie, considered all that gunplay a good thing because he didn't. David had long held the belief that America was far too violent for its own good.

"You going to let me stand one of the watches tonight?" Frank said.

"If you want."

"Figure I should do my share."

David glanced over at him again. "Plus I assume you wouldn't be real disappointed if we got a few intruders tonight and you had to have a little gunfight."

"No, brother, I guess I couldn't say that that would disappoint me a whole lot."

David moved his horse along the trail as long afternoon shadows began to form in the forests. The air was even cleaner and cooler now as the sky turned toward dusk.

"We should be near the Weller cabin now. We can pitch camp there tonight and then ride on in the morning." He tightened the reins on his horse. "You can take first watch tonight if you want, Frank."

Then he hastened his mount along, going on ahead to scout the terrain.

The first thing Abernathy had done after getting away from the Adams brothers was check his saddlebag to see if anything was missing. While the Mounties were certainly an honorable group of men, there were sneak thieves in every outfit.

Nothing had been taken.

His secret was still safe.

Now, seated on his fresh horse, still holding up the rear of the patrol, Abernathy wondered what he'd be doing right now if he were still living in the castle on the ancestral grounds. Abernathy's real name was Douglas Sims, Lord Douglas Sims to be exact, and he was a genuine British aristocrat who'd run away from home a year ago to prove to himself that he could be a man. Life around the castle was just too soft for him. Vast riches and eager servants made life too simple for a boy who'd dreamed of hard high adventure in some lost port of call. So at nineteen, under the name Abernathy, he'd joined the Mounties.

Lately, in a stray fit of homesickness, he'd written his younger brother, describing his life at some length. His brother, who had written back, had been thrilled to hear from Douglas and agreed to keep his secret. But the letter stated plainly, for any prying eyes, that Abernathy, who was supposedly the son of a millwright from Toronto, was actually British royalty.

Fortunately, his letter was safe and now, his headache nearly gone, his scarlet coat dusted off, and a beautiful sunset painting the land a combination of gold and shadow.

He was a proud Mountie, he was, with only one regret, that being that he'd yet to have the hard high adventures he'd dreamed of. He'd spent most of his first year working around Fort Cree, spending an undue amount of time on duties such as potato peeling and digging latrines. The youngest men always got such jobs.

Carmichael was looking around again.

Abernathy paused in his thoughts long enough to take note of this and to note that Carmichael seemed very nervous about something.

His eyes were always tirelessly scanning the piney hills around them, as if he were expecting an attack of some sort.

At first, Abernathy thought he might be wrong, that Carmichael was just displaying the same natural anxiety they all felt to some degree. The hills provided a perfect hiding place for outlaws and Indians alike.

But now, after a full day of watching his fellow constable, Abernathy knew that something was wrong here.

Abernathy wondered what.

He couldn't go to Sergeant Adams and say that he suspected Carmichael of anything—because what *did* he suspect him of? Strange as the constable's behavior might be, what did his gaping around mean in the end?

All Abernathy could do was keep a careful eye on the other man. And, to be honest, he rather liked that idea.

Suspecting that a fellow constable was up to no good was a lot better way of spending your time than peeling potatoes or digging a hole for somebody to piss in.

Ahead of him now, Carmichael started scanning the hills again.

Abernathy watched him closely. Having himself one hell of a good time.

• • •

Half an hour later the patrol came to the crest of a steep, grassy hill. In the valley below, cast in deep shadow now at twilight, they saw the lights of the Weller cabin, a substantial log dwelling complemented with outbuildings and a small corral.

Sergeant Adams, who was still at the head of the patrol, felt his stomach tighten. He had not seen Robert Weller since the man's terrible accident a year ago. He wasn't sure how he would handle himself around a once-robust and virile man who was now confined to a wheelchair.

Sergeant Adams raised his hand and waved the men down the grassy slope to the cabin.

His stomach still felt tight and vaguely sick as his mount found purchase on the dew-slippery grass.

Just what *was* he going to say to his old friend anyway?

chapter
five

AS THE PATROL DREW NEARER THE WELLER spread, the sounds of cows, chickens, and dogs sounded on the dusk air. The smell of woodsmoke came up from the cabin's chimney.

Sergeant Adams stopped his men when they were a good three hundred yards out from the place, told them to dismount and make camp for the night. This meant finding firewood and spreading out their saddles and blankets.

Frank Adams went with the constables.

David Adams went up to the door and knocked.

When she opened the door, standing there backlit in lampglow, he remembered just how beautiful she was. Louise Weller may in fact have been the most beautiful woman he had ever seen, a soft blond woman who even in gingham could look handsome.

Seeing David, she flung her arms wide and took him into a tight embrace.

He kept his eyes closed a moment, enjoying the sumptuous feel of her flesh and the lavender scent of her cologne.

When he opened his eyes, he looked over her shoulder and saw her husband Robert sitting in the middle of the single big room.

He was in his wheelchair.

"Hide the women and the booze! It's the Mounties!" Robert Weller called out cheerfully.

David walked into the house, his long boots making noise on the wooden floor.

He had known the Wellers since they'd immigrated here from Australia seven years ago. In that time, he'd probably spent sixty or seventy evenings out here, usually as he was returning to Fort Cree from an assignment. The three had become the best of friends, and David had been the godfather at their infant daughter's christening, a daughter who had later died of chicken pox.

Shortly after Robert's accident last year, David had used his three-day pass to ride out here and see his friend. But Robert had Louise bar him from the cabin. He said he didn't want his friend David to see him in this condition. He said he didn't, in fact, ever want to see his old friend again.

Many times after, David had been tempted to ride out here and tell Robert how foolish he was being. But somehow he'd never gotten around to it. Ultimately, he supposed he had to grant Robert his wish to be alone.

He looked at the man in the wheelchair now, and felt a great sorrow.

Robert had gained at least thirty pounds and much of his hair had turned gray. He was no longer the strapping young man he'd been. His accident had turned him into an old man and from the way he had slurred his words just now, David suspected that he was a drunken old man at that.

He walked over and put his hand out.

Robert slapped his own hand into David's and they shook. David winced. Whatever other powers Robert might have lost, his grip remained like steel. Many nights they'd arm-wrestled. David couldn't recall winning even once.

"God, it's good to see you," Robert said, his brown eyes looking the Mountie over carefully. He grinned, some of his old handsomeness coming back. "You still look great in that Mountie uniform, my friend."

Then, before David could say anything, Robert called out to Louise, "How about another glass of beer? And put a little whiskey in this one, would you?"

From the sink, Louise glanced over at David. Her expression said many things, all of them sad.

"And bring David some beer, too, will you, Louise?" Robert said.

"No, thanks," David said. "Technically, I'm on duty."

Louise came over and took Robert's glass. She filled it and brought it back.

"I see you brought other men with you," she said.

David nodded. "We're on patrol. Have to go arrest a man."

"Oh?" Louise said.

"Yes. Barton Jaeger."

Her expression changed abruptly. She seemed disturbed by his words. He couldn't imagine why. Barton Jaeger gave homesteaders like the Wellers just as much trouble as he gave the Mounties. Louise should look happy that the man was finally being brought to justice.

"He's a very tough man," Louise said. "He won't be easy to bring in."

"No, he won't. But we'll do it."

And then he told them about his father's murder, and his brother Frank coming up from Montana.

"I'm sorry about your father, David," Louise said softly. She looked more like the old Louise now. David still couldn't figure out why she'd looked so strange before.

"Thanks, Louise."

"Hope you get the bastard and hang him," Robert said. Even though he was addressing David, he was staring straight at his wife.

Quietly, another enigmatic but troubled expression on her face, Louise excused herself and went back to the sink.

Robert returned to his forced, beery joviality. "Well, sit down here and tell me what you've been up to, Mr. Mountie. We don't get much news out here in these parts."

So David did just that, sat down and brought Robert up-to-date on all the events at Fort Cree.

Every few minutes he noticed that Louise would sneak a quick glance at them.

He still couldn't make sense of her. He just knew that mention of arresting Barton Jaeger had troubled her in some way.

But why would Louise care about a man who should have been arrested and hanged years earlier?

• • •

Dinner was hardtack, dried buffalo meat, and coffee. Soon after, three of the men started playing cards by the flickering glimmer of the campfire, while two others slept early, heads back against the seat of their saddles, hats over their faces.

Carmichael had propped himself up against the base of a spruce tree and was whittling.

Abernathy sat across the fire from him and was reading a book by his favorite author, Sir Walter Scott. But he was also keeping an eye on Carmichael, whose gaze seemed just as nervous and furtive as it had back on the trail. Clearly, Carmichael expected something to happen to the patrol tonight.

Abernathy wondered what it was.

He was just starting to read again when the jangle of spurs brought his head up.

Frank Adams had returned to camp. He'd told Abernathy that he wanted to scout the terrain so he'd know what they were up against in case something happened.

He came over, knelt on his haunches, and poured himself a cup of coffee.

Frank Adams scared Abernathy a little. Where his brother David Adams was outgoing, open, and took pains to put you at your ease, Frank Adams almost never shared his thoughts and barely responded to even the most cordial of questions. Abernathy sensed a great and frightening turmoil in the man. He didn't want to be anywhere around if Frank Adams ever lost his temper.

Frank Adams sipped his coffee.

Abernathy put down his book. "Find anything interesting out there?"

"Not much." Frank shrugged. "Lots of good hiding places for bushwackers."

"You really think Jaeger knows we're coming for him?"

Frank nodded. "If he's like most outlaw bosses, he's got spies everywhere, including the fort."

Abernathy noticed that even though he didn't look up, Carmichael had started to squirm.

Could Carmichael be Jaeger's spy at Fort Cree?

In the lingering light of the fire, Frank's face looked as if it had been painted gold. "I'll take first watch tonight."

"Then I'll take second, if it's all right with you."

"Not me you have to worry about, son. It's my brother David. He's in command here."

Abernathy sat up, letting the fire warm his face and chest and shoulders. He sat Indian-legged. He wished the fire warmed his backside as well.

"I'm sorry about your father," he said.

"I appreciate that."

Abernathy nervously went on. Frank made him feel like a helpless, jabbery kid. "One good thing will come of all this anyway."

"What's that?"

"Barton Jaeger will be dead."

Frank sipped some more coffee. "I hope you're right, son."

"I don't see him giving up without a fight, do you?"

"Not from what I know about the man, no I don't."

Frank Adams stood up. Even in boots, he wasn't very tall. He sure was a contrast to his brother, Abernathy thought again.

"Well," Frank said, "guess I'll make another pass over by the horses. See how they're doing."

"You need any help, you let me know."

Frank nodded and moved away.

Behind him, Abernathy heard a snicker and then, " 'You need any help, you let me know.' "

Abernathy spun around and saw Carmichael, still whittling, sneering up at him.

"Well, what's wrong with that?" Abernathy said.

"I'm sure a lawman like Adams needs the help of a pup like you."

"Who said I was a pup?"

Carmichael laughed. "I did. You want to do something about it?"

Abernathy was aware that the others had quit playing cards and were staring at him now.

He had been challenged. What was he going to do?

He wasn't afraid of Carmichael—even if the older man could whip him, it wouldn't be by much—but he was most definitely afraid of Sergeant Adams, who would not appreciate at all the spectacle of his men rolling around on the ground and taking pokes at each other. This was the sort of thing that could land on your permanent record.

Abernathy looked down at Carmichael and shook his head. "You think you'll ever grow up, Carmichael, or will you always be a punk?"

And with that Abernathy risked walking away, which meant turning his back on Carmichael.

One, two, three, four steps. Abernathy waited for the other man to jump to his feet and come after Abernathy. But nothing happened.

When he got to the edge of the firelight, everything else darkness except for the star-filled sky, he heard Carmichael say to the other men, "I'm gonna take care of that sonofabitch one of these days. You wait and see if I don't."

Sergeant Adams was starting to feel guilty. Here he was in a snug cabin warming himself in front of a fire while the others were outside in the chilly night. This was the fastest way possible to lose the respect of your men.

He said, "Well, Robert, I guess I'd better be heading back to my men."

"You're welcome to sleep on the floor here."

"Afraid that's not a good idea. Not when my men are sleeping on the ground."

Robert, who was drunk enough now that his head sometimes bobbled on his shoulders, leaned forward and nodded to Louise.

"She's been lookin' at those damn photographs again," he said. There was a hint of drunken malice in his tone.

Louise looked up. In three-quarter profile, she was stunning, every feature perfect. "Robert resents it when I look back on our Melbourne days."

"What's the use of lookin' back?" Robert said.

"Pleasant memories, for one thing," Louise said softly.

David Adams saw the trouble here. Louise wanted to retreat into the shelter of memories, of golden sun-filled times in Melbourne that memory had rendered perfect. Those days hadn't been perfect, of course, no days ever are. But for Louise, memory had become a cloak with which to warm herself. And Robert resented her. He could not escape his present—his body dead from the waist down—and he did not want her to escape the present, either.

David felt sorry for both of them.

He stood up. "Really, I've got to be going." He looked around the cabin. "You always did have a nice place."

Robert looked at him drunkenly. "You haven't said a damn thing about it."

"Oh?" David said, trying to keep his voice cool yet cordial. He knew what was coming. His stomach was in knots once again. "About what?"

"You know damned well about what, David. My god-damn legs."

Louise stopped washing dishes, froze.

"I figured I'd like you to bring up the subject, Robert."

"Well, then, I'm bringing it up."

Robert was drunk enough that he sloshed beer across his shirt as he hoisted his glass to his mouth.

He took a long drink.

Louise looked over at David. She looked humiliated.

Robert took the glass from his face. "You like having a cripple for a friend?"

"Guess I don't think about it much one way or the other."

"Well, I guess it's a little easier on you than it is on her," Robert said, nodding to Louise. "Considerin' that I can't be a man for her anymore."

"Robert!" Louise snapped, turning from the sink to face him. "David doesn't want to hear all this."

"Well, if he's my friend, then it's about goddamn time he *did* hear all this as far as I'm concerned."

"Robert—"

David held up his hand, walked back to Robert.

He put a hand on his friend's shoulder. "I don't imagine I'd accept the accident any better than you have, Robert.

I'd be bitter and angry, too. But there's one thing I wouldn't do—or hope I wouldn't anyway."

Robert's head was down as David talked.

Now Robert looked up, bitterness apparent in his face. "And what would that be, Mr. Mountie?"

"I wouldn't take it out on a fine woman like Louise."

"Oh, you wouldn't, huh?"

"No, I wouldn't."

"Well, what if I told you that maybe Louise isn't as fine a woman as you might think?"

Louise looked at David and shook her head. She walked straight to the front door and stepped outside, slamming the door behind her.

"She hasn't got that coming, my friend," David said softly.

"Yeah, well, you sonofabitch, did I have *this* coming?" Robert shouted.

And with that he hurled his beer glass across the room where it smashed against the wall and fell in silver fragments to the floor.

Robert put his face in his hands and began sobbing.

chapter
six

PRINE'S FRIENDS WERE THE ANIMALS AND THE forest. If he wanted to know where the man he was tracking had gone, then an animal would give him a sign, or a tree, or the wind. And he would soon enough pick up the man's trail again.

Prine had been moving fast since Jaeger had told him to kidnap Frank Adams.

Now, moonlight guiding his way through the long grasses sowing in the wind, he came to the crest of a hill and looked down upon the Weller place.

It looked almost smug, so snug and peaceful against the night.

Not far away he saw where the Mounties had camped.

A fire lit the faces of the young constables. One of them played a mouth harp, a sentimental tune the white men had brought with them from Europe. Prine preferred the lament of the barn owl, or the song of the robin.

He moved farther down the hill, hand wrapped tightly around the hilt of his brutal, bloodstained knife. He never cleaned it after use—whether on man or animal—because he wanted the steel of it to absorb the soul of the thing he'd just killed.

The closer he drew, the more he could hear the Mounties talking and laughing. How young they sounded, many Mounties in this part of the territory barely meeting the mandatory age of eighteen.

But for now, Prine was interested in only one man.

He stood beyond a spruce tree, peeking out for a better look, ready to take flight at any given moment.

He stared down at the men around the campfire.

One of them was Frank Adams, the man Barton Jaeger had paid him to bring back as a hostage. He had not known until this afternoon how much Jaeger hated the Adams boys. But that would make sense, Jaeger's brother being in prison and all.

The night was just beginning.

Before he made any move on the man, Prine had to isolate Frank in some way. Not even Prine could fight nine men.

He would isolate him and then render him unconscious and take him away.

He crept even closer down the grassy hill, pausing behind a spruce tree for a better look.

Only one man lacked a Mountie uniform. That had to be Frank. The man's size surprised Prine. He looked nothing like his tall, slender, blond brother.

Now he at least knew what Frank looked like.

Now Prine could begin to make his plans.

Ever since the accident that had cost him his legs, Louise Weller had been given to crying jags that her husband seemed to have no influence over.

Nothing could stop her crying.

She sat now in the rocking chair in front of the crackling fire, rocking softly, staring into the snapping flames, silver tears rolling down her lovely cheeks.

He hated to admit it, but her tears made him feel good.

If he had to suffer from his accident, then she should suffer, too.

He sat in his wheelchair by the table, a fresh glass of beer in his hand. His own crying was done for the night. His own crying had forced his friend David Adams out the door. Weller felt vaguely ashamed of this, now that he was sobering up some, but he kept sipping beer so the alcohol would dull any embarrassment he felt.

Finally, unable to endure her silence anymore, he said, "I didn't mean to embarrass you in front of David."

"Well, for not meaning to, you certainly did a very good job of it."

"David understands how tough I have it."

She turned now and looked at him. "How tough you have it, Robert? Has it ever occurred to you that maybe I have it tough, too?"

"At least you have your legs."

She stared at him a long moment, her gaze implying that he was entirely missing her point, and then she turned back to stare into the fire.

He waited a long time to say this but finally, after a few more sips of beer, he leaned forward and said, "You been sneaking out and seeing somebody."

He saw the way his words jolted her, as if somebody had just poked her with a sharp stick.

But she didn't turn around. Didn't meet his eye.

"Did you hear me?"

"I told you before, Robert. You must be dreaming."

"Dreaming, hell. I saw you and I heard you. I want to know where you went those times."

She said, still staring into the flames, "Haven't we argued enough tonight, Robert? I'm weary of it. I just want to go to bed."

He sipped more beer. "You snuck out to meet somebody, didn't you?"

Nothing; she said nothing.

"Who is it you've been sneaking around to see?"

"Ever since your accident, Robert, you've been imagin-ing—"

"Imagining nothing. That's what you want me to think. 'Poor old drunken Robert. He just imagines things.' Well, I know better, Louise. I know damned well better!"

He slammed his glass so hard against the table, it sloshed beer all over his arm.

She started sobbing again, quietly, this time her whole body shaking.

Frank stared into the fire. "Sounds like your friends are having some problems."

David nodded. "His legs. He's not taking it very well."

Frank sighed. "Doesn't sound like she's doing a whole lot better herself."

For a time the men were silent, just watching the fire, staring up occasionally at the starry night, listening to the soft snoring sounds the young constables made sleeping around the fire.

Every few minutes there'd be a sound from the cabin, Robert's anger or Louise's sorrow.

It was sad to hear and robbed the crisp night of some of its beauty.

Finally, Frank said, "Well, I'd best be making the rounds."

David smiled. "You always did hate to sit still, brother."

Frank laughed. "Even when we were little boys I hated to sit still."

"Especially when we were little boys, Frank. You even went out in the rain to play."

Frank looked at him. "While you stayed inside and read your Sir Walter Scott novels."

David showed him a leather-bound he held in his fingers. "Still am reading Scott, matter of fact, brother."

Frank stood up, stretched. He bent over and poured himself the dregs of the coffeepot. He drank as much of the bitter dregs as he could choke down, then splashed the rest of it off into the weeds.

He leaned down and picked up his Winchester.

"Guess I'll be headin' out," he said.

"I'll take the second watch," David said.

Frank nodded to the sleeping form of Constable Abernathy. "He said he'd like to have it."

"That's one thing you can always count on Abernathy for."

"What's that?"

"Enthusiasm."

Frank looked over at the young man. "Well, that's something that comes in handy every once in a while, brother."

With that, he hefted his Winchester and went to meet the darkness.

• • •

Constable Abernathy had heard every word.

Even though his eyes were closed, his mind was wide awake.

He lay on his side so he could sneak a look at Carmichael every once in a while.

Abernathy sensed that, like him, Carmichael was playing possum, too.

Abernathy lay there listening to the fire crackle and pop and to a wolf cry lonely in the darkness.

Pretty soon now Carmichael would be making his move.

And young Constable Abernathy would be ready.

From the bluffs, Prine watched as Frank Adams threw out his coffee, picked up his Winchester, and started back to where the horses had been bedded down for the night.

It wouldn't be long now.

Prine was excited.

Except for the times he spent with the Fallon girl, nothing thrilled him like stalking someone.

He moved down to a copse of silver birches for a closer look at Frank Adams.

The U.S. Marshal was headed over to the horses.

Where David had always liked books and education, Frank Adams had always pursued the outdoors, and especially the company of horses. He liked horses so much, in fact, that he'd spent days at the library reading about them, how even before man there had been horses on the North American continent, as proved by fossil remains. But the horses—along with most other living creatures—had been destroyed by the Ice Age and did not reappear again on this particular land mass until thousands of years later when Cortes and other Spanish conquerors brought them into Mexico, where the Mexican Indians feared the animals so much that they literally ran away in terror whenever they encountered one of the creatures.

Frank stood downhill of the horses now, listening to the small, warm animal noises they made as they slept. They seemed to stir and dream in their sleep very much like humans.

Frank crouched down low and petted one of the animals on the crest of her head. She made a grateful little sound.

And then Frank heard it.

At first he wasn't even certain what it was.

Just some tiny sound that shouldn't have been on the night.

He rose to his feet, holding the Winchester tight, getting it ready.

Prine knew that Frank was aware of him now.

Not so dumb for a white man, Prine thought, begrudgingly paying the U.S. lawman a compliment.

Frank stood in a clearing next to the horses. Moonlight made him a silhouette. His Winchester gleamed in the soft light of night.

Prine drew closer, closer, his knife ready.

It would take great force to take this man hostage.

Frank tried the east edge of the forest first. He wanted to find out what had made the noise. He suspected it had been a man.

The horses had heard it, too. They were awake now, a few of them standing up in that odd way of horses that was both graceless and graceful.

Frank kept searching, his eyes trying to penetrate the darkness that was deepened with both moonsilver and shadow.

He knew he was getting nearer, though; soon he'd find his man.

Prine had been touched by the way the lawman had knelt down and stroked the sleeping horse. The gesture told Prine a great deal about the tenderness inside the harsh man, and it also told him of the harsh man's vulnerability.

Prine knew exactly how he would force the man to entrap himself.

• • •

Frank Adams heard the horse cry a few minutes later.

The sound was unmistakable: a horse in pain of some kind, a noise that was part suffering, part panic. Horses frightened even more easily than humans.

The horse's cry coming from somewhere behind him, Frank spun around, his Winchester ready.

Prine did not enjoy giving the horse pain. But he had no choice. He had to lure Frank Adams out here.

He kept hold of the horse's ear, pulled back just enough to inflict pain, pulled back just enough to make the animal cry.

Prine walked the horse into the great meadow east of the campsite, the moon-touched grass looking like a vast silver ocean now.

He kept close to the line of forest, so that he and the horse were lost in the shadows.

He paused then, giving the horse's ear one last tug so that the animal would cry out once more.

As he did.

Then Prine stopped. And waited. Frank Adams would be along soon.

Adams wondered what could make an animal sound this way. So hurt. So desperate.

He hurried, not quite knowing where he was going, the guiding sound lost occasionally on the night wind.

He came to the crest of the hill, his Winchester tugged into his arm, his finger near the trigger.

He knew this could be a trap, a diversion to lure him away from the campsite.

But he would be less than a man if he put his own safety above that of a vulnerable animal's.

He reached a great silver meadow and heard the wind play in the long grasses.

Once more the horse cried out. Frank Adams turned in that direction, over along the shadowy timber line.

He had gone six steps exactly when someone leapt from the darkness and grabbed him with incredible strength and threw him to the ground.

He smelled an Indian and felt the cold steel of a knife at his throat.

And then the Indian brought a great rock down upon Frank Adams's skull and the white man knew only tremendous pain and then total darkness.

chapter
seven

ANNE FALLON WAITED UNTIL HER FATHER HAD
drunk himself to sleep and then she crept from their small
cabin on the edge of Barton Jaeger's stockade.

She bore, in her small white hand, a long letter on a single
piece of plain white paper. She had spent the entire night
writing it.

The letter was addressed to Prine and it told him in great
painful detail how much Anne Fallon loved him, and how
she did not care that he was half Indian, that she would run
away with him anyway.

That was their only hope, running away.

She had grown up in Jaeger's stockade, lived here all her
nineteen years, daughter of an outlaw, her mother having
died when she was only ten.

If she stayed here much longer, her marriage hand would
be claimed by a whiskey runner named Dubois, a man who
followed her around constantly, and who spent a good deal
of time at the cabin plying her father with cheap whiskey
and promises of what a good husband he'd make for Anne.
By now, her father trusted Dubois completely, and told Anne
frequently that he expected her to marry the man, and soon,
and bear him children. Even outlaws grew older and wanted
grandchildren and that's where her father was at this point
in his life.

Two sentries walked the night.
She had to make certain that they didn't see her.
Everybody in the stockade suspected that she and Prine

were in love and none of them approved of it.

Getting caught sneaking into Prine's wigwam would only confirm this.

She kept to the shadows, passing pathetic lean-tos and pitiful tin shacks and a few log cabins that housed snoring men and crying babies. This was an entire settlement here, not just the outlaws themselves, but their hard-scrabble families, too. She had always thought of it as the poor white man's version of an Indian reservation.

Prine's wigwam was in sight now.

Her heart beat faster.

Just the thought of leaving the note for him—of telling him how much she cared for him—excited her.

She came to a jarring stop.

A sentry passed her not ten feet away.

She clung to a cedar tree, pressing tight against it, thankful she'd worn a dark green shawl on this cool night, one that offered her some protection from curious eyes.

Jingle of spur; spit of tobacco juice; the sentry passed on, finishing his sweep of this end of the stockade.

She hurried now, fast through the shadows to the wigwam.

In the moonlight, it looked forbidding, dark, and somehow threatening. She could see where dew lay on its stretched animal hides, silver drops of dew like pearls.

She wished she could throw back the flap and find Prine inside.

She could feel his strong arms around her, hear his deep but curiously gentle voice in her ear.

She took the letter from inside her dress, ready to throw back the flap of the wigwam and place it inside.

She glanced quickly around, careful that nobody watched her.

Confident that she was safe, she bent over, turned back the flap, and leaned inside the wigwam.

She placed the letter, folded in half, directly in the path Prine would take.

It lay there in the gloom like an emblem of truth and beauty and rapture. She could not wait for him to read it.

She was just starting to stand up when somebody grabbed her hair from the back and pulled her roughly erect. The pain in her head was overwhelming. She felt as if the person had ripped handfuls of her hair out by the roots.

The man spun her around and slapped her so hard across the mouth, she fell sideways into the doorway of the wigwam.

Then he grabbed her by the shoulder and jerked her toward him.

"You little whore, what're you doing in there?"

He clasped her arms so tightly, pain shot up and down her muscles.

"It's none of your business, Dubois," she said.

"If yer gonna be my wife, it's damn well my business, 'specially since it concerns that breed."

"His name is Prine."

"Prine!" Dubois said. A big man, with the wild beard and wild gaze of an Old Testament prophet, he wore a pioneer hat, a sheepskin vest, a rough-hewn work shirt that probably hadn't been washed in three weeks of wear, and gray trousers that carried every kind of stain possible, from animal's blood to oil.

She couldn't stand to look at the filthy man, let alone let him put his hands on her.

He tightened his grasp. "You put somethin' in there, didn't you, you whore?"

"What I do is my business."

She knew she should be trying to settle him down not rile him up but she was furious that he'd followed her over here.

Now he pushed her aside and pushed his way into the wigwam.

A moment later he reappeared, the white letter in his filthy fingers.

He waved the letter in her face. "What's this say?"

She couldn't help herself. She smiled. "I forgot, Dubois. You don't know how to read, do you?"

He grabbed her arm again. This time he worked extra hard at inflicting pain.

It worked. Her eyes teared up as she stood there, feeling as if her arm had been snapped in half.

"I want you to tell me what this here says!"

With her good hand, she tried to snatch the letter back from him.

But he raised the white sheet above her head, making her jump up and down for it as if she were a small child he was teasing.

"Give that to me! It's mine!"

He laughed, a hard, cruel sound in the darkness.

"I haven't been doing anything except being his friend," she said.

He snorted. "Next time I see him, I'm gonna kill him. You tell him that for me."

"You leave him alone!"

He pushed her away. She bumped against the wigwam again. The entire structure shook.

He waved the letter at her again. "You're gonna be sorry you ever wrote this, you whore. You understand me?"

And with that, he stormed off.

Ten feet away, he paused and looked back at her. "You just wait till you hear what your pa says when I show him this letter."

He shook his head, cursed, and walked away, the letter dangling from his right hand, white in the moonlight.

She stood there humiliated, enraged, and frightened. Prine was strong and fast but she didn't know if he was as strong and fast as Dubois.

So far as she knew—at least if her pa was to be believed—Dubois was the toughest man in the stockade.

chapter
eight

SERGEANT DAVID ADAMS CAME AWAKE KNOW-
ing instantly that something was wrong.

The fire had guttered low. The cabin downslope was dark
except for curling gray smoke from the chimney. The sounds
were of the night; an owl, a coyote, a dog somewhere. And
somewhere in the distance, their horses.

His men were all asleep. There was soft, wet snoring,
rolling this way and that to get comfortable.

He stood up immediately, throwing off his blanket with
one hand and grabbing his Snider carbine with the other.

According to his pocket watch, his brother Frank should
have been off first watch an hour ago. But he hadn't come
back to wake anybody.

He tried to convince himself that Frank just preferred
duty to dozing.

But he kept moving quickly now, past the flickering
remains of the fire, up into the dark hills surrounding the
encampment.

He spent the next half hour looking for his brother. He
went west as far as the rocky ravine, as far east as the chill
waters of the Cree river, as far south as the long grasses
where the horses were bedded down for the night.

It was there, not far from the horses, that he found sticky
blood on the grass. The blood was still warm.

He could see, from where the grass had been beaten down,
that some kind of struggle had taken place here.

And his brother Frank had lost.

Otherwise, how else could you explain his vanishing?

Convinced now that Frank was in great trouble, David went back down to the campsite and woke the men up.

They struggled to consciousness with varying degrees of success.

David had started a fresh pot of coffee for them. He poured while he explained that Frank had somehow been abducted.

"Jaeger?" one of the men said.

"Who else," another replied.

"We'll get him back, sir," the youngest of the constables said to David.

David smiled grimly. "I appreciate your fervor. But it won't be as easy as you might think. They have a head start on us and if they reach the stockade first—" David shrugged. "It won't be easy storming the stockade. Not with just the eight of us."

"How were you planning to get in there anyway, sir?"

David pointed to his saddlebag. "I've got an arrest warrant in there. I planned to serve it. But with Frank as a hostage—" He shook his head. They had a few hours' ride to the stockade and he wanted to get going.

He hadn't had time to think properly, to formulate anything resembling a plan. He had always prided himself on his ability to stay cool and rational even in the darkest moments—but losing his father to Jaeger . . . and now having his brother stolen—

He pawed at his jaw and said, "Let's get ready and move out."

He didn't know what he was going to do yet. All he knew was that he wanted to get to the stockade and he'd worry about it then.

Frank Adams had been hit so hard he didn't regain consciousness for fifteen minutes.

His wrists and ankles were bound tight with rope and he was slung over a saddle.

The horse he was on trailed behind the horse rode by a half-breed who turned back to check him every few minutes. He recognized the mount as one belonging to the Mounties.

The half-breed had stolen it. He suspected the half-breed was taking him to Jaeger's stockade, which meant he would have to endure this rough ride for another few hours.

They were on a rocky upslope, working their way between some scrawny lodgepole pines.

"Who the hell are you?" Frank said.

It was not easy talking, slung over a saddle this way, but he needed to orient himself.

The half-breed just looked back. He had an imperious face and a dark, angry gaze. He looked to be enjoying Frank's dilemma.

The half-breed turned away from Frank, then kept giving his horse a little rein to make it up the rocky slope.

Frank stayed silent.

His head pounded from where he'd been hit, sticky blood having trickled down the back of his shirt.

When they reached the peak of the hill, Frank saw below a plain that was almost breathtaking. Long grass swayed in the breeze. Several buffalo grazed to the north and several wild horses to the west. To the east a low fog, forming just now at dawn, gave the region a dreamlike feel, its cottony tatters stretching all the way to the horizon line.

But Frank knew he wasn't entering the land of an enchanted kingdom. Hardly. This was all land controlled by Barton Jaeger.

The loss of blood and lack of sleep had left Frank dehydrated. He badly wanted a drink of water. Through parched lips, he told this to the half-breed.

The man seemed not to hear. He didn't turn around, didn't cock his head to better hear the words, he didn't slow their pace.

But a few minutes later the half-breed suddenly stopped his mare and jumped down.

From his saddle he took a canteen. He brought it back to Frank.

It wasn't easy giving Frank water pitched across a saddle this way but the half-breed worked at it till he got it right.

Then he capped the canteen and went back to his mount. They resumed riding.

After a while Frank started getting curious about the half-breed.

He didn't think he'd ever met anybody this silent. Outlaws tended to be braggarts and bullies who liked to lord themselves over you. And God knew the half-breed was in a position to do that, what with Frank bound up the way he was.

But the man said nothing at all.

Just kept riding toward some point over the horizon that he alone knew.

Frank was adding another name to the list of people he definitely planned to kill when he reached the stockade. Barton Jaeger was first. The breed was second.

Frank's horse picked its careful way among the timber. Frank, his chest and back aching from his awkward position, ground his jaw muscles and daydreamed about having his arms and legs free and a gun filling his hand.

chapter
nine

LOUISE WELLER FOUND HER HUSBAND WHERE
she usually found him, slumped over in his wheelchair.

The time was just at dawn.

She had awakened because of the noise she heard uphill,
where the Mounties had encamped for the night.

She went over to Robert now, taking a blanket with
her.

It was a wonder he didn't have more colds. Most nights
he drank beer till he passed out in his wheelchair. And
slept the night through without anything more than a shirt
on his back.

Looking down at the man now, she felt a great deal of
pity for him and hated herself for feeling it. He didn't
want her pity, he wanted her love. But that was the one
thing she could no longer give him. His bitterness following the accident had destroyed her old feelings for
him. Where before he'd been a bright, happy man, he
was now dark and violent. She was afraid that even in
his wheelchair he'd sometime lash out at her physically
and hurt her.

She put the blanket over him and leaned down and tenderly
kissed his tousled hair.

All she could do was pray that he never found out about
her relationship with Barton Jaeger, a relationship that had
started one day when, quite by chance, they'd met on a
dusty road after her wagon slipped a wheel off.

He'd come along in a buggy, a big, handsome, self-
confident man and she'd felt herself enthralled before she

knew who he was. But by the time she learned his true identity—though Barton Jaeger was infamous in this part of the country, few people had seen him—she was already captivated.

He'd begun his odd courtship by coming to the edge of the forest north of their homestead and making the sound of a black crow. Curious, waking up in the middle of the night, she'd gone to the window to see what could possibly be disturbing a crow this much, and there, silhouetted against the full round golden moon, she'd seen Barton Jaeger, looking as fine and heroic as the lead actor in a stage melodrama.

She'd gone to him that night and many nights afterward. Her secret became her shame but her secret also became something else—her only possible escape from the bitterness and abuse of her husband.

And now Robert was aware that something was going on with his wife.

He couldn't put the exact words to it yet, but it was something he could sense.

She wished she could talk to him about it—tell him that she'd changed her mind about Jaeger ever since he'd killed David's father. She'd known then that no matter how handsome and charming Barton Jaeger was, he was every bit the ruthless killer people said.

But how could she tell Robert? And could he ever forgive her her foolishness with Jaeger?

She had just finished buttoning her dress when the knock came.

She went to the door and opened it.

David Adams stood there, dressed in his uniform looking grim.

"What happened?" she said, stepping back so he could come inside.

Once over the threshold, he looked over at Robert in the wheelchair.

"I know it's not easy for you," David said. "Maybe he'll be more accepting of what happened as time goes on."

She touched his arm. "You're a good friend to both of us."

He nodded and then said, "Somebody abducted Frank. I don't know how it happened but he's gone. Obviously somebody from Jaeger's stockade."

"My God," she said.

At the name of Jaeger, she felt her cheeks color. She hoped David couldn't see in the dim, dawning light. "You're sure it was Jaeger?"

"Had to be. Nobody else would have a reason."

"I suppose you're right."

"We're going after them. I figure they've got about a two-hour head start. Maybe we can catch them."

Louise said, "I wish there were something I could do."

David nodded. "Give Robert my best. Tell him I was glad to see him."

"I'm sorry about the scene."

David looked over at his friend. "I'm not sure I'd be any better handling it than he's been."

"It took his self-respect. That's the worst part."

She had tears in her voice and eyes. She hated her life now. Poor Robert—and then making things worse by betraying him with Jaeger.

And then she got the idea. Only one person had any chance of reasoning with Jaeger, of convincing him to let Frank go.

She did.

She would have to tell the truth both to Robert and David but certainly it would be worth it to save a life—perhaps many lives.

She opened her mouth and said, "David, there's something I need to tell you—"

But then behind her, she heard Robert grumble to life. He had an empty beer glass on one arm of the wheelchair. He picked it up and hurled it against the wall, shattering it into shards.

And then he collapsed back into his troubled sleep.

And for Louise, the moment was gone, her courage evaporated.

"What were you saying, Louise?" David asked.

But all she did was shake her head and fight back tears. No, maybe it was for the best that nobody else knew of what she'd done.

Knowing the truth would only destroy Robert and lose her any respect she had coming from David.

"Nothing, David, I was just going to say take the trail that heads southwest. It's the fastest way to Jaeger's, I'm sure."

He offered her a sad smile. "I'll do that, Louise."

He leaned over and kissed her tenderly on the cheek.

"Things will get better here," he said softly. "I'm sure of it."

That was so much like David—at a time of his own trouble, thinking of her trouble, too.

"I appreciate it, David," she said, and then watched as he turned, going out the door.

After a few minutes, she heard horses being saddled and then mounted, and the party of Mounties taking their leave.

She quietly closed the door and then looked back at her husband.

He was now twisted pitifully in the wheelchair, wide awake and glaring up at her.

"You and David seem to be getting pretty fond of each other," he said.

He wanted to say more but before he could she began sobbing uncontrollably.

The sounds she made were so violent that he was forced into bitter silence.

Dubois had gotten up this morning with only one intention and he took care of it immediately.

He staggered out into the stockade yard, tugging on his filthy shirt and running a hand through his gnarled black hair.

A rooster was just crowing, announcing dawn.

From various huts and lean-tos came the smell of breakfast cooking, mostly raw meat seared black enough to eat without causing illness.

Dubois looked around, making certain that nobody was watching, and then he stumbled on toward the east edge of the stockade, taking with him kerosene he'd poured into a pail.

Prine was not back yet.

This would be easy.

Dubois went into the forest that nearly touched Prine's wigwam and retrieved a giant armload of kindling.

He put the kindling just inside the wigwam's doorway and then doused it with kerosene.

He was bending over the kindling, getting ready to strike the match, when he felt something metal prod the small of his back.

Even in his hung-over condition, he recognized the business end of a gun poking his flesh.

"What the hell you think you're up to?" Dubois said. He had no idea who it was. He didn't care.

"Pick up that kindling and take it down to the creek."

"You really scare me all right, you little whore."

"You heard what I said."

The hell of it was, Dubois had suddenly started believing the bitch would actually shoot him.

Just to save the wigwam of that goddamn breed.

He tried turning suddenly and knocking her down with the sheer force of his elbow.

But she was quick, and ducked, and this time, now that he was turned around, she shoved her .45 right up near his face.

"It would give me pleasure, Dubois. And you'd better believe it."

She kicked dust in the direction of the kindling.

"You pick that up and march it down to the creek."

He thought of pouncing on her but he had to admit that for now, anyway, she definitely had the upper hand.

"You little bitch."

"Save the sweet talk for later. For now, just pick up the kindling."

So he obliged her.

After a few minutes, he had an armload of kindling that stank of kerosene.

"Now move."

So he moved.

And as he moved, he saw that his worst fears had come true.

A dozen or so stockade folks were standing in the center yard watching and listening to Anne Fallon boss him around.

Dubois felt the unaccustomed heat of a blush burn his cheeks.

Little bitch. She'd pay for this. She'd pay for it real good as soon as he got his chance.

He walked down to the creek, stood on the edge.

She marched right behind him, the .45 held at the ready. "Now throw it in."

Behind them, the stockade folks were coming down to the creek now, too. They didn't want to miss any of this. Hard to believe anybody—especially a dinky little woman like that Anne Fallon—could hornswoggle a man like Dubois.

She prodded his back with the gun.

"Bitch," he said under his breath.

And then he threw the kindling out into the water.

For a creek, the water was wide and fast. The current picked up the kindling and immediately started sailing it downstream.

A nearby frog watched all the action, seeming to enjoy it just as much as the stockade folks did.

Dubois turned around. Faced her.

"Keep those hands up," Anne Fallon warned.

Some of the women watching snickered; it was always fun to see a bully get his.

"Now," Anne Fallon said, "you march right back to the wigwam and get that kerosene out of there."

A woman applauding did it, tipped Dubois over the edge. Even if it meant him getting shot, he couldn't take this kind of humiliation anymore.

He jerked forward suddenly, trying to slam the .45 from Anne Fallon's hand.

Unfortunately, when he leaned, he put himself off balance, so even a woman as small as Anne had an easy time of pushing him backward straight into the creek.

Dubois, giant that he was, made a huge silver splash as his form hit the water.

Everybody gathered around, including Anne, knew better than to be there when Dubois resurfaced.

"You'd best run and hide, missy," and old crone called to Anne.

"Come to my cabin," another older woman said, "and I'll hide ye beneath m'porch."

Hearing Dubois starting to struggle up out of the water, Anne thought hiding beneath somebody's porch was a right nice idea.

She took off running.

chapter
ten

CARMICHAEL WAS DOING IT AGAIN.

The patrol had been on the trail for all of the morning and half of the afternoon now, Constable Abernathy taking the rear position as usual, and Carmichael was almost constantly doing it again.

Scanning the hills as if he knew for certain somebody was up there, scouting or waiting.

Abernathy recalled Frank Adams' comments at Fort Cree about Barton Jaeger having a spy inside the fort.

Was Carmichael that spy?

Why else would the man be looking around so often?

Abernathy decided that now was the time to tell Sergeant Adams of his suspicions. He was tired of keeping such a secret to himself.

He spurred his mount and galloped past the other horses on the narrow, dusty trail.

As he passed by Carmichael, he saw that for the first time the man wasn't looking around the hills. Instead, Carmichael was staring directly at him. Hostility burned in the man's eyes.

Abernathy spurred his mount once again.

He drew abreast of Sergeant Adams, reined his mount in, and fell into the even trot of Adams's animal.

"Afternoon, Constable. You have some news?"

Abernathy glanced back over his shoulder.

Carmichael was still looking at him, glaring.

Did Carmichael know that he'd been found out? Or did he

merely think that Abernathy had caught up with the sergeant simply to curry a little favor?

"Did you hear me, Constable?" Adams said.

"Uh, yes, sir."

"I asked if you had news."

"Right, sir."

Adams looked irritated now. "Well, do you?"

"Uh—"

And Abernathy glanced back over his shoulder again. At Carmichael. Who looked, in this particular moment, like a very innocent Mountie who was simply riding along the trail doing his job.

Now that he was actually alongside Sergeant Adams, Abernathy realized that he didn't really have much evidence to present.

He's been looking around the hills a lot, sir, Abernathy would say.

Isn't that what I told you men to do, Constable, keep a careful eye out, Adams would say.

Well, yes, sir, but you see, sir, it's—

It's what, Abernathy?

Well, he looks at the hills *more* than he should and—

More than he should?

Yes, sir, you see and—

In panic, Abernathy said, "I just wanted to report that everything's all right at the rear, sir. No sign of savages or outlaws."

"*That's* what you wanted to report?"

"Yes, sir."

"That's all, that's the whole thing?"

Abernathy at least had the grace to bow his head. "Yes, sir."

Sergeant Adams stared at the other man for a good long time. Clearly, something was wrong here. Abernathy had come up here with every intention of telling him something.

But what?

And why had he so abruptly decided not to tell him?

"Abernathy."

"Yes, sir."

"Look at me."

Abernathy raised his head. "Yes, sir."

"What did you really want to tell me?"

And once again, Abernathy felt this real urge to tell him but he'd only look stupid, and snitching this way would only get him in badly with the other constables. Nobody liked a snitch.

"That's really what I wanted to tell you."

"Get back in line."

"Yes, sir."

"And, Abernathy?"

"Yes, sir?"

"I expect that sometime soon you'll tell me the real truth."

Abernathy looked desperately at his commander again and rode back to his place in patrol.

Corporal McKenzie looked at Sergeant Adams and said, "I wonder what that was all about, sir."

David Adams looked just as curious as McKenzie did. "So do I, Corporal. So do I."

The stockade was bigger than Frank Adams had anticipated.

Even in late afternoon, sentries were posted on the three corners he could see. Jaeger was no fool. He expected trouble.

Other than the sentries, however, the stockade looked like any other village.

Children ran alongside barnyard animals in the big center yard; women in gingham dresses bent over spring gardens; a smithy banged away at shodding a horse; and somewhere somebody played a fiddle.

The air smelled of meat cooking for the supper hour.

Prine rode in, trailing the other horse behind him.

Shouts went up. Virtually everybody in the stockade stopped what they were doing to get a look at Prine's trophy.

The half-breed rode slow and easy through the stockade all

the way up to Jaeger's cabin. The easy gait allowed children to run alongside the hog-tied figure of Frank Adams. It also gave the adults time to gawk at him and point and grin.

A big man appeared from nowhere and stopped Prine from going any farther.

"Out of my way, Dubois," Prine said.

Frank was surprised to hear anger of this kind in Prine's voice. While not everybody in a stockade got along, this kind of near rage was curious.

"I get him first," Dubois said.

Prine didn't know yet about Dubois's humiliation at the hands of Anne Fallon. Dubois needed some way to impress the people of the stockade again. When he saw Prine bringing Frank Adams in, he saw his opportunity.

Before Prine could say anything, Dubois walked back to where Adams was slung over the horse.

"Well, Frank Adams," Dubois said. "You don't remember me from down in Montana, do you?"

"Sure, I do, Dubois. I couldn't ever get the smell out of my clothes."

Somebody snickered.

Dubois hit Adams on the side of the head.

Frank Adams saw black swimming before his eyes.

"Leave him alone," Prine said. "I brought him here for Jaeger, not you."

Dubois looked up at him. "I thought maybe you brought him here for Anne. That's why you seem to do everything else, you goddamn injun."

"Leave Anne out of it."

"You'll regret puttin' your slimy paws on a white girl, believe me."

Prine moved his horse again, across the wide dirt yard, white chickens scattering as he approached, right up to Jaeger's cabin.

Prine dismounted and went up the steps and knocked.

Jaeger came out, cigar in his mouth, pinkie ring twinkling in the dying sunlight. He looked more like a riverboat gambler than ever.

He came down off the steps and walked over to Frank.

"Well, well," he said. "It's the man who put my brother in prison."

He leaned closer. Peered at blood trickling down from Frank's ear. "I was watching out the window, Frank. Dubois really gave you a good one, didn't he?"

Jaeger nodded to Prine. "Get him down from there."

Prine silently set about his task.

Frank was so dizzy from the long ride that he nearly collapsed when Prine stood him upright.

Prine took out a knife and cut away the rope around Frank's feet. He left the bonds around his wrists.

Jaeger came over and stood in front of Frank, enjoying his cigar as he eyed the lawman.

"By tomorrow morning, I reckon I'll have your brother here with me, too," Jaeger said. The anger was evident in his voice and eyes now. "He'll come to fight for his brother just the way I'm fighting for my brother."

"Your brother's where he belongs," Frank said.

Jaeger smiled. "I almost forgot. You're the hothead. Your brother's the reasonable one." He took a drag from his cigar and let the smoke out slowly, in a billowy cloud. "Now your brother wouldn't have said that. He would have just let my remark pass. He wouldn't have told me that my brother belongs in prison at all. But you—you are a hothead, aren't you, Frank?"

Jaeger slapped him then.

It was a blow so quick and so hard that Frank felt he was going to fall over backward. He'd been tied up and deprived of sleep too long to have much strength left.

Hot blood trickled from his nose and mouth.

"Stick around, Frank," Jaeger said. "The fun's just starting."

He nodded to Prine again. "Why don't you take our friend Frank over to the post and put him there."

Prine shook his head. "He's an honorable man, Jaeger, he doesn't deserve the post."

Jaeger's eyes narrowed and then he laughed. "He's another hothead just like you, Frank. And a breed to boot." He looked abruptly at Prine. "Now understand me, boy, I don't give a damn what you think. I want him tied to the post and I want him tied now. We understand each other?"

Prine grabbed Adams and led him away.

The post was at the west end of the stockade. It turned out to be just about what Frank expected.

In many settlements of mountain people you found one place where somebody who had displeased the majority was tied up as a form of penance. Usually this was a post and the person was bound hand and foot. But that wasn't all. Before being put there, a large area circling the post was dug out. Into this hole people poured garbage of every kind, often even emptying latrines into it. The smell was literally enough to knock some people out. And there was one more little pleasantry. In addition to rawhide to cut your wrists and ankles, and in addition to sewage so foul many people threw up on the spot, the children of the village or stockade had the right to not only taunt but to throw rocks at the person being punished. Adults were forbidden this singular pleasure, but virtually anything the children did was fine.

Now, as Prine moved him along the yard toward the post, Frank saw that the setup was the same here.

Women in gingham bonnets and gingham dresses were already emptying garbage into the hole.

It wouldn't be long now before somebody came back with a couple buckets of excrement from the nearby latrine.

chapter
eleven

IT WAS A BAD ONE TODAY, A VERY BAD ONE, and so Louise Weller went to work.

She had to help Robert outside so he could vomit, and then she had to help him back inside so he could drink cool water, a few careful swallows at a time. Every so often all the alcohol he poured down himself caught up with him, and today was such a day.

But today she did something she never did.

She went over to the kitchen cupboard, took down a bottle of whiskey, and poured him two large shots in a glass.

She brought the glass over and handed it to him.

"What's this?"

"Whiskey."

"What happened to all the temperance speeches you're always giving me?"

She shrugged. "I see how miserable you are. I just thought this would help."

He studied her beautiful face suspiciously. "You're up to something."

"My God, Robert, I try to be nice and look what I get."

He hoisted the glass. "This doesn't make any sense. Not coming from you it doesn't."

She made a pass with her hand to take the glass away from him. "Then I'll pour it back into the bottle. Will that make you feel better?"

"I just want to know what you're up to."

"I'm not up to anything."

He stared at her. "You've become a deceitful woman, Louise."

And with that, he tilted his head back and poured about half the glass down his throat.

When he was finished, he said, "Today I want you to tell me."

"Tell you what?"

"About the nights. About where you go when I wake up and find you gone."

She shook her head, started to walk away.

His hand shot out and grabbed the back of her dress. "Today," he said, "I want the truth."

"Leave me alone, Robert, and let me do my work."

She jerked away from his hold and went back to the sink and counter.

Behind her, he sat looking out the window. She always wondered what he thought about at such times. Was he thinking of what it would be like to have legs again and be able to move at will among the beautiful things of the forest? Probably, because in the days before his accident, Robert had spent a great deal of time hunting for mushrooms and exploring old Indian trails and riding the rapids in a canoe some Cree had given him.

Once again, she felt a terrible pity for him.

She just wished she could still feel love.

He took the rest of the whiskey.

She could hear him behind her, sighing as the searing liquid went down his throat and into his belly.

A few more drinks like these and he'd be well on his way to passing out.

And then she could sneak off.

She'd already decided to intercede on behalf of David's brother Frank.

There had been enough heartbreak in her life these last few years. She did not want to see her family friend—who'd just had his own father murdered—go through yet another tragedy.

She knew she could convince Jaeger to let Frank Adams go.

"Gimme another one," Robert said behind her.

She didn't turn around to look at him.

She simply walked over to the cupboard, took the bottle down again, and then brought it over to him.

She poured.

"More," he said.

She poured again.

"More," he said again.

She hated herself for doing this. Robert was quite consciously killing himself. He didn't seem to have the courage for putting a shotgun in his mouth but he did seem to have the patience for the slower, self-degrading death of alcoholism.

He grabbed her wrist. "Just leave it here."

"You'll start bleeding again if you drink all this. Maybe you should switch to beer now."

"I don't want beer. I want whiskey. And I want you to leave the bottle here."

"You're hurting me."

"Then let go of the bottle."

"I'm just worried about you."

He looked at her and scowled. "You're so worried about me you sneak off in the middle of the night and meet somebody."

He tightened his grip on her wrist.

Her fingers let go of the bottle.

He snatched it from her grasp.

"Now get the hell out of my sight," he said, turning his chair to the back window where he liked to sit and stare out at a leg of the creek where deer came to drink.

Deer were his favorite animals. He got positively sentimental about them, which always surrprised her and let her know that even in the embittered, present-day Robert there was some tenderness left.

She went back to her tasks.

Dusk was beginning to paint the sky a darker hue, and here and there stars shone brightly.

It would not take him long, not on whiskey, and he would be out for a good long time.

She could easily get to Jaeger's stockade and get back before Robert awoke from his nightly stupor.

"I wasn't kidding, Louise."

His voice snapped her out of her thoughts. "What did you say?"

"That I wasn't kidding."

"About what?"

"I want to know who you sneak off to see at nights."

"Just drink, Robert. Just drink and be quiet."

"One way or the other, you're going to tell me. I promise you."

He took another deep drink and moments later she heard the clink of the whiskey bottle against his glass.

Oh, yes, Robert would have himself a fine time today.

The Indian attack came just before Sergeant David Adams and his men reached a parallel run of timber that rose in subtle undulations to the foothills. Meadowlarks, sparrows, and blackbirds soared on the spring air.

While most of the Indians in this part of the country happily abided by treaties, some of the younger braves spent too much time with the whiskey traders, and sometimes fell to war with any white man who represented official authority. And Sioux as well as Cree fought Chippewas and Stonies in roaming warring bands.

These Indians missed "the old ways" as they called them, the days before treaties when both the plains and the timbers belonged to them, when buffalo meat supplied not only food but fuel, dried dung being one of the principal fuels. Buffalo also contributed clothes and shelter as well.

There was a movement among some young Indians to return to the old days—the days even before horses were used when hunting—when brave Indians hid beneath bison robes or wolf skins so they could get very close to their prey.

Now there were whole tribes in the States that had to suffer the indignity of getting their meat on beef ration day at the white man's fort, where beeves, after being rounded up, were packed together in corrals and shot by turncoat redskins known as "Indian policemen."

David Adams first saw the three Indians on the crest of the grassy hill above them.

The Indian in the middle, riding what appeared to be a calico, leveled his rifle and squeezed off two quick shots.

He didn't come within fifty feet of hitting Adams.

The young Mounties in the rear of the patrol were frightened. "We'd better take cover, sir," one of them shouted when he saw that Sergeant Adams was sitting tall and proud in his saddle, and showed no inclination whatsoever to dismount or move.

"Sir?" asked Corporal McKenzie anxiously. "Hadn't we better do something?"

And just then two more shots *panged* off a boulder. But these shots were just as bad as the first two had been.

Adams frowned to himself. He had no time for games, not with his brother's life hanging in the balance, but he knew he had to take care of this situation and quickly.

"Wait here," he said to his men.

"But, sir, you can't—"

Adams drew his Snider carbine from his scabbard, spurred his horse, and took off riding up the hill toward the Indians, his scarlet jacket bright against the darkening sky.

The middle Indian, seeing Adams approaching, lowered his carbine until it was pointed directly at the Mountie's chest.

"You go no farther, redcoat."

But Adams kept riding straight ahead.

Now the Indian on the right also raised his rifle and pointed it directly at Adams's chest.

"I say the white man die," this Indian said.

But still Adams kept riding, right up the hill, right to the Indians.

When he reached them, his Snider resting across his saddle horn, he said, "I'm Sergeant Adams."

"Mountie," said the third Indian.

"Yes," Adams said, "a Mountie. That's something to be proud of as far as I'm concerned."

The Indians grunted and looked at each other. Up close, none looked to be more than sixteen or seventeen. They were boys, really, and not men at all. In their war paint they looked threatening enough, he supposed, except for their eyes, which conveyed the tension they were obviously feeling.

"Did you hunt the moose this spring?" Adams asked.

"Why you care?" the middle Indian asked.

Adams smiled. "Because I went moose hunting once and I didn't do well. I just hoped you might have had better luck."

Obviously, they kept waiting for him to get angry or belligerent, but that wasn't the way of a thoroughly trained Mountie.

The Indian on the right, a chunky boy in hide clothing, said, "I use the moose call. Trick the moose."

Adams had seen the device the youth referred to, an old-style birch-bark horn that deceived the moose into believing a mate was calling him.

The middle Indian said, "I shot the moose."

"I'm envious," Adams said.

He started to raise his Snider. Instantly, they raised their three weapons.

He held the Snider up so they could see it and then he quickly put it back in his scabbard.

"If you killed a moose," he said to the Indian in the center, "then I wonder why you couldn't hit me when you were shooting at me."

The Indian glanced anxiously at his two friends. "Wind not good today."

"Oh, I see," Adams said, "it was the wind, eh?"

Adams knew what had happened, of course. The brave had been showing off for his companions. He did not want to actually kill a Mountie but he wanted to pretend that he tried to, thereby earning the esteem of all outlaw Indians.

But this Mountie had surprised him by riding up here to talk.

The Indian looked nervous. Obviously, he didn't want to talk about the shooting anymore. "Quanto want know why came up here," the Indian said, keeping his horse from nuzzling the animals on either side.

Adams obliged him and changed the subject. "You know Barton Jaeger, I believe."

The Indians scowled. All Indians knew Jaeger. He was the cruelest of white men. Some of his outlaws had killed Indians from time to time, and raped Indian women.

"Know Jaeger, yes."

"How would you like to help me put him in prison?"

"In white man's prison?"

Adams nodded.

"Hate Jaeger."

"So do I."

"Why you hate him?"

Adams looked straight at Quanto. "He killed my father."

"The man the gods appointed to be your protector on this earth?"

"Yes. And now I want to put Jaeger in prison for doing it. And I'd appreciate your help."

Quanto looked at the other two. "We are not many. Jaeger's men in stockade are many, many."

"You can help me in another way."

"How?"

"I want you to pay a visit to Jaeger tonight."

"Quanto visit Jaeger?"

"Yes."

"Why?"

"So you can sneak me inside. A white man could never get inside the stockade. But an Indian could."

Quanto looked again at his two friends. "Quanto just shot at you."

"Yes."

"You not angry?"

"Right now I'm more angry with Jaeger than you."

"And you want Quanto to help?"

"Yes." He pointed down to his men, each of whom was looking uphill earnestly, their Sniders held at the ready.

"They want to shoot Quanto."

"Not if Quanto agrees to help," Adams said.

"How Quanto get you in stockade?"

Adams pointed to his men again. "We will first forge the river and then make camp. Then I'll tell you about my plan. You're welcome to join us in some food."

Quanto said something to his friends in Cree, something that Adams didn't understand at all.

The other two Indians laughed.

Adams sensed that he'd just been insulted.

But now wasn't the time for vanity.

For his plan to work, he really would need the cooperation of Quanto, and if that meant cooperating with a man who basically hated him, so be it.

It would all be worth it to see Barton Jaeger behind bars in territorial prison.

Now the three braves quit smiling and began muttering to each other, again in Cree.

After a time Quanto looked up and said, "You know what they think?" he said, indicating the other two.

"What do they think?" Adams said.

"They think you crazy if you not try to shoot me for me trying to shoot you."

"Well, maybe that's my trouble," Adams said, "maybe I am a little bit crazy."

The Indians laughed again, and looked at him with hooded eyes and smurking mouths.

Five minutes later they followed him down the hill and joined his patrol.

chapter
twelve

FROM THE POST WHERE HE WAS LASHED, FRANK
Adams watched the stockade settle into evening.

Torches appeared, and lanterns. The smell of braised meat
filled the air. The voices of mothers seeking out missing
children sounded both irritated and slightly desperate.

So far, Frank had suffered the following indignities: two
boys, approximately ten years of age, had come over, grinned
up at him, and then spat on him till they couldn't work up
any more spit; a grown woman had come along, looked
him up and down as if she were examining an animal at
auction, and then threw a bucket of rotted vegetables into
the shallow pit surrounding the post; and then an old man
with one eye and no teeth appeared and kept talking to
him in a language Frank took to be some kind of Creole.
He didn't understand a word of it. The old man just kept
giggling and spitting tobacco. Fortunately, he didn't spit
any on Frank.

Now, Frank stood in the evening, his wrists and ankles
raw from the rope that bound him, his senses filled with the
filth that lay at his feet. About every twenty minutes or so,
somebody brought more excrement and poured it into the
pit and went away laughing.

From what he'd seen of the people here, they were
about what you'd expect to find in an outlaw stockade—
uneducated, physically filthy, perhaps even a little crazy.
The frontier in both the United States and Canada was rife
with such outposts and such people. Some of them, even a
lawman could feel sorry for. Some of them, simply, should

be hanged. The excuse that they were "underprivileged" didn't hold with Frank. A lot of people on the frontier were underprivileged but they didn't become outlaws because of it. They put their backs to plows and made little homesteads for themselves and raised decent families.

She was so small, he didn't even see her come up. Her dark dress made her almost invisible against the night.

"Hello."

He just looked at her. This could easily be a trick. Pretend to be nice to him and then throw something filthy in his face.

"My name's Anne."

Still, he just watched her.

"Can't you speak?"

"I'm just waiting to see what you want."

"I brought you some beef broth. Aren't you hungry?"

Indeed, he was. Even with the vile smells of the pit filling his nostrils, his stomach grumbled.

"Yes, I guess I am."

"I can feed you."

"Why?"

"Why what?"

"Why would you feed me?"

"Because I don't like what they're doing to you."

"Will you take some of the broth?"

"Will I?"

"Yes."

She laughed. She sounded intelligent and somehow that comforted him. "You think it's poison?"

"That's always a possibility."

"You really don't trust people, do you?"

"Look where I am. Smell the air. Would you trust people?"

"No, I guess not."

She came up closer to him. He could see her scowling as the stench overtook her.

She held the cup up to her face and from the folds of her dress produced a small spoon.

"Watch," she said.

In the soft starlight, he saw her dip the spoon into the cup and take some broth. She put the spoon to her mouth and took in the broth.

"There. Are you satisfied?"

"I still don't know why you'd do this."

"Because I don't like to see men suffer." She leaned even closer and said, "I just hope The Chosen don't see me."

He was just about to ask her who The Chosen might be when she shoved a spoonful of warm, tasty broth into his mouth.

As Frank Adams was taking his first nourishment in more than a day, Robert Weller was just starting to wake up from his stupor.

The first few minutes were always the worst. You weren't sure where you were; sometimes you weren't even sure who you were. Your body was dehydrated and you wanted to vomit but you didn't know if you had the stamina.

He sat in his wheelchair in the center of the cabin. It was completely still except for the night sounds of jays and crickets and a distant dog. The only illumination was soft moonlight through the few windows.

In his lap was the whiskey bottle. Empty.

He let it fall to the floor. It made a loud, lonely sound when it reached the boards.

His head pounded.

There'd been an argument, he was sure of it. At these times, he always wanted to apologize to his wife because whatever she'd done, she didn't deserve the way he treated her. But then, the longer he was awake, the more he started to blame her for what had happened.

Now, he called her name.

It became one more night sound, lost in the tides of darkness.

He called her name again.

For a moment he had the sense that he was utterly alone in the entire universe.

He wheeled himself over to the counter, where the beer and corn liquor was kept.

He got himself a beer. His stomach knotted as he first began swallowing the stuff but after two or three swallows, it started to taste good. Even this little of the liquid was starting to make him drunk again. He felt better, safer, more confident.

After pouring himself a large glass of beer, he wheeled over to the cabin door, opened it, and looked out.

Hard to believe twenty-four hours had passed since Sergeant David Adams had been here. He vaguely remembered a scene of some kind with his old friend, shouting at him or something. Well, David would understand. It wasn't easy for a rugged, independent man to lose his legs. Not easy at all.

He had been assuming that Louise was around here somewhere. That she'd just gone for a walk somewhere, as she sometimes did.

But then on the hill, silhouetted against a full moon, he saw the dark shape of rider and horse. The way her long hair flew behind her, he knew it was Louise.

But where was she going riding so fast?

What had happened during his time of blackout that would cause his wife to ride off this way?

He started shaking, then his entire body was caught up in an uncontrollable tremor.

The huge silver disc of moon was empty now, rider and horse having disappeared behind the long, waving grasses.

He sat there staring at the moon and feeling again that he was the only person alive in a universe that made no sense at all.

After a time, almost because he didn't know what else to do, he bowed his head and began crying softly.

"Is it good?"

"Very good. But let me ask you a question."

"What?"

"If somebody sees you feeding me broth, won't they get mad?"

"I suppose. But the damage is already done. The broth's in your stomach."

And with that, she quit feeding him.

"I appreciate this."

"It's all right." She hesitated. "He didn't hurt you, did he?"

"Who?"

"Prine. The half-breed."

"No."

"He wouldn't. Not while you were tied up, anyway."

When she started speaking about Prine, her voice changed. This made him curious about their relationship. "He's the only man with any honor in this whole stockade."

"He hit me with a rock and abducted me."

"You're a white man."

"There isn't much I can do about that."

"White men have treated him horribly."

"How about Jaeger? How has Jaeger treated him?"

She sighed. "Just well enough to keep him working for him. Prine doesn't exactly have a lot of job opportunities."

"Jaeger's already killed one lawman, my father. If he kills me, that's going to make two—and Prine'll be involved in this one."

"I'm going to talk to him in a few minutes. I'll do what I can. I promise."

"Thanks for the broth. That was brave of you and I appreciate it."

She shook her head. "I just wish there was something I could do about the stench."

And with that, she retreated into shadow again. After a moment he couldn't see her at all, just hear the rustle of her dress as she walked quickly back to her cabin.

chapter
thirteen

BY THIS TIME, CARMICHAEL KNEW THAT SOME-how, tonight he was going to desert.

The Mounties, in general, had problems with deserters, of course.

For every fair-haired boy who found the RCMP a romantic and fulfilling adventure, there was another who saw it as nothing more than a bleak, hazardous, boring job. And so they ran away. Sometimes, this was understandable. A boy found that one of his parents had died back home, and he got so lonely he couldn't do much else but go back and visit his brothers and sisters. Or a boy met a girl and wanted to marry her but there was insufficient time for her if he wanted to stay in uniform. So, like the others, he ran, too. And then there were welchers, young men who ran off in order to flee debts they owed the whiskey traders for gambling. Or owed one of the fort merchants for such items as condensed milk, sardines, and tinned fruit.

And now Carmichael was going to become one of these deserters, too.

He thought of all this as he scouted the land near the river's edge for kindling. Sergeant Adams had dispatched him to build the night's campfire.

His arms loaded now, he started back to where the horses were being fed and rubbed down for the night.

He saw Constable Abernathy half jump behind a tree, obviously worried that Carmichael had seen him.

What was going on? Carmichael wondered, irritated.

Abernathy had been watching him closely all day. Did Abernathy suspect something?

Had Abernathy somehow figured out that Carmichael had given information to Barton Jaeger?

He passed the tree where Abernathy hid.

His impulse was to throw the kindling and logs down and jerk Abernathy out from behind the tree.

There was something about Abernathy he didn't like anyway, something a bit too polished for his tastes, almost as if Abernathy had been high-born or something.

But Carmichael told himself he was being foolish.

In another few hours he would be gone, headed for Dawson or Skagway, someplace he could get lost for life, with the Mounties unable to find him.

He went into the camp, knelt down, and proceeded to light the fire.

In a few minutes flame leapt from the logs he'd piled up in a V, and the pleasant smell of woodsmoke joined the clean night air to make the Mounties hungry.

Svensen, who was the patrol's unofficial cook, set about making the meal.

Carmichael got to his feet, wiped off his hands, and then turned around to look out at the moonlit river.

But as he turned, he saw that somebody was standing not far away, watching him.

None other than Constable Abernathy himself.

Carmichael shook his head, then looked out on the peaceful river.

At first, Frank Adams couldn't be sure what the people were up to.

They appeared out of the gloom, the men bearded and in filthy rags, the women scruffy in tattered dresses, and they stood around him in a semicircle. Each person held a flickering torch that stank of kerosene. He remembered what Anne Fallon had started to say about The Chosen.

Nobody said anything. Just stared at him.

Frank stared back.

He had no idea what these folks were up to but he assumed

it wasn't going to be anything he'd like.

Finally, one man spoke.

"Do you want to be cleansed?"

"Cleansed?" Frank said.

"Your soul, pilgrim."

The man talking stepped out of the semicircle, closer to Frank.

He had long, filthy hair, a white beard that reached the center of his chest, and he walked with the help of a crutch. He wore a ragged shirt and some kind of fur vest. "Do you know who we are?"

"No."

"We're God's People."

Frank looked around at the solemn, crazed faces watching him. "I see."

"We do his bidding."

"Must be a pretty nice job."

If the man noticed the sarcasm, he didn't let on.

"The fire does not lie."

"The fire?"

And with that, the man extended his torch. Flame flapped inches away from Frank's face; the smell of kerosene was so strong, it overcame even the smell of feces at his feet.

"It never lies."

"The flame?" Frank said.

Before the other man could answer, a booming laugh sounded from the surrounding darkness.

Gradually, the form of Barton Jaeger took shape as he stepped from the gloom into the flickering light of the torches.

"I see you've met Brother Edmund," Jaeger said. He looked, as always, like a riverboat gambler who'd just run into a considerable amount of luck.

Frank nodded.

"And he's told you about the flame?"

Frank nodded again.

Now, Jaeger glanced over at Brother Edmund. "Are you ready?"

"Oh, yes, Brother Jaeger. The Lord personally spoke to

me earlier. He said to find out the truth about this man. And all eight of my followers are ready to help me."

Jaeger smiled. "I'll bet they are."

Jaeger turned back to Frank. "I let these people stay here at the stockade and in return they help me keep the peace among the others. Sometimes he comes in quite handy. Isn't that right, Brother Edmund?"

Brother Edmund made an eerie noise that resembled a cackle. "Oh, yes. Folks don't give you any trouble when they know that you're acting in the name of God."

"I don't imagine they do," Frank said, looking at Barton Jaeger.

At the moment Frank didn't care if he lived or died especially. He just wanted one full minute with his hands around Barton Jaeger's throat.

He'd even put up with such outright lunatics as the pathetic Brother Edmund—clearly a deeply insane man— and his followers.

Barton Jaeger stepped back from the torchlight, back into the shadows again.

"Proceed, Brother Edmund," he said.

Brother Edmund stepped forward and pushed his face into Frank's. His breath was at least as foul as the feces at Frank's feet.

"You know the truth of the flame, pilgrim?"

"I guess you'll have to tell me."

"Those who tell the truth it does not hurt."

"I see."

"But those who lie—well—the flame hurts."

And with that, Brother Edmund reached into his shirt pocket and produced something small and dark.

He quickly closed his hand around the object.

"Do you know what it is?"

"Guess I don't," Frank said.

"It is a vessel of the Lord's."

"I see."

"The Lord wishes me to use it to demonstrate the truth of the flame."

"I see."

Around him, the eight followers began rumbling their approval.

"Watch," Brother Edmund said.

His hand came open. In the center of it was a small brown field mouse.

It looked cute and helpless against the filthy palm of Brother Edmund's hand.

"Are you watching?"

Frank nodded.

"Because the mouse cannot speak, we must rely on his essence alone. If its essence is good, then it will survive. If its essence is bad, it will perish."

And with that, Brother Edmund put his hand out to one of his followers.

The follower dipped his torch down.

The flame found the mouse.

The tiny animal let out a chilling scream as its entire body was seared. It leapt from Brother Edmund's hand to the ground, where it ran off into the darkness, its entire body still enveloped in flame.

Many of the followers laughed.

"Not pure," one of them said.

"A sinner," said another.

Yes, Frank thought, you've got to be careful of those sinning mice.

But he knew that his situation was no joke.

By now, he knew just what Brother Edmund had in mind for him.

Brother Edmund stepped forward again.

"We are going to rip your shirt away, pilgrim, and burn your chest. If you are pure, then you will not scream as the mouse did."

And somewhere in the darkness beyond, Barton Jaeger said, "I told you that Brother Edmund comes in handy from time to time."

Jaeger sounded quite happy.

chapter
fourteen

CARMICHAEL SAT ON THE EDGE OF THE CAMP-
fire, watching, for the right moment when to flee.

If he waited till too late, sentries would be posted and
they would undoubtedly catch him.

But if he went soon, there would still be activity and he
could just pretend he was going into the forest for some
reason. And simply not come back.

He had managed to pick up the information about how
Sergeant Adams's new Indian friends were going to sneak
him into the stockade.

Carmichael would sneak into the stockade first and tell
Barton Jaeger this, and Jaeger would certainly pay him some
money for his information.

And then Carmichael would head for Dawson or Skagway,
and eventually set sail for San Francisco.

As a younger man, when he'd been a sailor, Carmichael
had spent time in the bay city and had been impressed by
the number and quality of the whores. He had never seen
such beautiful women nor such an abundance of them, either.
They came in all shapes, sizes, and personalities. And ages.
Carmichael had once slept with a fourteen-year-old girl who
claimed—and here he'd laughed in her face—that she was a
virgin. The only thing that he didn't like about San Francisco
were the cops. The bay city went out of its way to recruit the
biggest, meanest men they could find, and then equipped
them for all-out battle. Many drunken sailors, out on a
spree, found themselves in the sober morning missing eyes
and fingers and, in a few cases, noses. Because in addition

to huge pistols and huge nightsticks, the city fathers saw fit
to give their coppers foot-long knives, which they carried
in special sheaths on the front of their uniform coats for
easy access. Many coppers came to prefer their knives to
their other weapons because they were more reliable than
the pistols and more frightening than the clubs. At least
one copper, in a fit of rage, was known to have sawed
off a sailor's head with his knife, and many coppers had
sawed off sailors' hands. But even given that, Carmichael
liked San Francisco because of all the dives and all the
girls and all the fancily dressed hoodlums who ruled the
streets every bit as much as the cops did. These hoodlums
were always fun to watch, many of them taking girls right
there in the dives, right out in public, or hurling coins
at the barmaids to set up all the sailors with drink, or
getting into endless bloody battles with each other that
were always fun to watch as long as you didn't have to
participate.

Carmichael sat and stared at the fire, his memories as vivid
as pictures in a book, when somebody said, "We need some
water here, Carmichael. How about you hauling a couple of
buckets?"

Carmichael looked up and saw Sergeant Adams standing
over him.

Carmichael jumped to his feet. "Yessir."

Sergeant Adams handed over two buckets. Carmichael
took them.

He had to force himself not to smile.

Talk about luck. Here was the exact excuse he was looking
for to leave camp and wander off.

He'd take the buckets down to the creek and never come
back.

Before he left camp, however, he checked to see that he
had everything he needed.

His pistol. A few dollars. A hand compass in his pocket.
He would like to have taken his Snider carbine along, of
course, but that would be too obvious.

He felt eyes on him suddenly and looked up.

On the other side of the fire, Constable Abernathy sat. His

head was poked down into the small leather-bound book he was always reading.

Had Constable Abernathy been watching him?

Carmichael decided he was probably imagining things.

Hefting the buckets, he stepped over the forms of two men who had dozed off just after eating, and headed down the grassy slope to the creek.

Once away from the firelight, he felt much more secure.

He had always liked the darkness, the sense that you could move about without anybody knowing.

Halfway to the creek, he set the buckets down in the long grass and then took out his compass.

He held it up, reading it by moonlight.

The stockade was southwest from here, he knew.

He got a reading and then turned back to the camp for one last look. He was not going to miss the Mounties. It was too much hard work for too little pay.

Still, he felt a little bit of sentiment when he saw how the firelight glowed on the vast prairie, and heard the soft sweet harmonica music being played around the campfire.

But deciding he was being foolish, he shook his head and set off in a southwesterly direction, looking up at the full moon that was almost silver tonight.

He had gone ten full minutes before he thought he heard something.

He swiveled around, pistol filling his hand.

Behind him, all was long prairie grass waving in the silver moonlight.

No sign of anybody. Or anything.

Still, even when he resumed walking, he didn't put his gun away. He kept it in his hand.

He went only five minutes this time before he thought he heard something.

Again, he turned around, looked back.

And saw nothing.

What was spooking him so much? Was his guilty conscience playing tricks on him?

Shaking his head in disgust, he started to turn forward again and that's when he heard the voice.

"Stop right where you are."

Carmichael froze.

"Drop your gun."

The voice was clear, familiar.

The voice belonged to Constable Abernathy.

But where was he?

And then from the long grasses, Carmichael saw a dark human shape struggle up into the moonlight.

Constable Abernathy, of course.

Obviously the man had followed him.

"Going to see your friend Jaeger?" Abernathy said.

Carmichael said nothing.

"You still haven't dropped your gun," Abernathy said. He had his Snider pointed directly at Carmichael's chest.

Carmichael dropped his gun.

Always imaginative, Carmichael's mind was already filling with images of prison life.

He'd heard stories about how former Mounties were treated behind bars.

He shuddered.

"I don't know what the hell you're doing, Abernathy. I just went for a walk."

"And left the buckets behind."

"I was coming back to get them."

"Then you won't mind explaining all this to Sergeant Adams, will you?" Abernathy waved the Snider. "Now march."

Carmichael sighed, shook his head, and started walking back in the direction of camp.

Every few feet or so, Carmichael would calculate his chances of breaking running without getting shot.

Unfortunately, he always came to the same conclusion.

His chances weren't very good.

He marched. He went through the long grasses and then through the low, swampy area and then up the sloping hill leading to camp, with the eager, clean-cut Constable Abernathy always right behind him, his Snider very formidable in his hands.

Carmichael's mind kept filling with prison images.

He was getting scared. He would never survive life behind bars and that's just what he would get if Sergeant Abernathy could prove desertion.

So he decided to risk it.

He had no other choice.

They were coming up the hill, the long grasses having given away to earth muddy with spring, when he pitched himself forward.

Constable Abernathy did just what Carmichael had figured he would. Abernathy fired his Snider.

The gun blazed and bucked and roared in the night.

And on the ground, Carmichael kept rolling.

That was his plan. In the darkness, Abernathy wouldn't be able to find him for the first few moments, and he would probably empty his Snider shooting at where he imagined Carmichael's shadowy form to be.

So Carmichael kept rolling back down the hill.

He heard and felt bullets go whizzing by his head but he kept rolling anyway.

And then he heard the sweetest sound imaginable: the clicking of an empty Snider.

Young Constable Abernathy had run out of bullets.

Now Carmichael scrambled to his feet and hurled himself at Abernathy before the younger man could draw his revolver.

Carmichael smashed a blow into Abernathy's jaw and followed it quickly by slamming a fist into his solar plexus.

Abernathy started to sink to his feet, no match for the quicker and considerably meaner Carmichael.

When Abernathy was safely on the ground, Carmichael leaned over and snatched his revolver from his holster.

"You shouldn't have followed me," Carmichael said.

He could see Abernathy on the ground in the moonlight. Abernathy looked terrified.

Carmichael raised the gun and pointed it directly down at Abernathy's chest.

"You'd better say your prayers, this is the last chance you're going to get."

In the distance, Carmichael could hear the Mounties

starting to run from the campsite down the hill.

Carmichael had to be quick.

"You're going to shoot me?" Abernathy said, sounding like a ten-year-old.

"That's right, Abernathy. I'm going to shoot you."

"But—but—you're a Mountie and Mounties are honorable men."

"They are, are they?"

"You took the oath, Carmichael. The same as me."

Carmichael almost pitied him. Stupid young naive little bastard.

He pulled the hammer back on the revolver.

He could see Abernathy squeezing his eyes shut, getting ready for the shot.

At least he had some dignity. No whining. No begging. Just waiting to die.

"Take care of yourself, Abernathy," Carmichael said.

And shot the young man right in the chest.

Moments later, the shouts of the other Mounties growing closer, Carmichael set off for Barton Jaeger's stockade.

chapter
fifteen

BROTHER EDMUND, STILL BEARING HIS TORCH, took two steps closer to Frank and then ripped his shirt away.

An excited giggle went up from several of his followers.

Brother Edmund waved the torch above his head and then looked up to the night of the sky.

"If this man is pure, O Lord, give us a sign."

His followers, in unison, said, "Amen."

Behind the followers stood the other people of the stockade, including Dubois and Barton Jaeger. Both men looked greatly amused.

Brother Edmund lowered his head and stared at Frank.

"If you have been a defiler, then you will feel great pain when I put this torch to your chest."

Frank spit in his face.

A low murmur rumbled through the crowd.

Brother Edmund stood only a few feet from Frank, his face glistening with Frank's spittle.

"You are a devil," Brother Edmund said.

He sounded, as always, quite calm and quite crazy.

It was then Frank saw two members of the sect suddenly begin to struggle with somebody.

All attention was focused on them.

Even Brother Edmund turned around, forgetting Frank momentarily, to watch as Anne Fallon tried to wrest herself from members of the religious sect.

Finally, Brother Edmund said, "Let the woman go."

Reluctantly, the two men who'd been wrestling with her complied.

Anne Fallon jerked away from them and walked up to Brother Edmund.

"You have no right to do this," she said.

She was furious.

"I am the way of the Light and the Lord," Brother Edmund said, hoisting his torch again. "And this man is a devil."

"He is not a devil," Anne Fallon said. "He's just a man— and an innocent one at that."

And with that, Barton Jaeger himself stepped forward.

His nose wrinkled when he came in contact with the smell of the pit.

He looked at Anne Fallon and said, "I wouldn't call him innocent, Anne. He sent my brother to prison."

"That still doesn't mean he should be treated this way."

"Then how should he be treated, Anne? How would you feel if somebody put your brother in jail?"

Anne shook her head. "But to torture him—"

Brother Edmund, crazy as ever, shook his head. "This is not torture. This is finding out the truth."

Now Anne turned to Jaeger. "Please don't let him do this. You know it's not right."

Dubois had been watching all this. He broke from the crowd now and stalked over to Anne. "Let Jaeger alone. This is his stockade."

Anne looked as if she wanted to say something more to Jaeger but Dubois grabbed her by the wrist then and slapped her viciously across the face.

"You come with me," Dubois said, "and I'll teach you how to act around white men."

And with that, he grabbed her wrist again and started to pull her to him.

But suddenly a tall, lone figure appeared from nowhere and seized Dubois around the throat.

A long knife blade was put to Dubois's throat as Anne stumbled away from his grasp.

Prine's grip on Dubois was so tight that the bigger man was gasping for air. His face was bright red. His eyes bulged.

Then Prine pushed the white man away and went into his fighting crouch, his blade still flashing in the firelight.

Jaeger tossed Dubois a knife.

Dubois took a few minutes to compose himself after nearly being strangled to death.

The two men kept circling each other.

By now, the stockade had forgotten all about Brother Edmund and Frank.

In fact, even Brother Edmund was watching the fight, setting his torch at his feet and looking as goggle-eyed as any youngster watching the adults go at each other.

Dubois inflicted the first cut.

He half leapt forward and slashed his knife across Prine's shoulder.

Blood came immediately.

The crowd gasped, thrilled.

But if the pain of the cut had any effect on Prine, he didn't let it show.

He went back into his crouch and started circling again.

"Get the breed, Dubois!"

"Cut the breed, Dubois!"

"Kill the breed, Dubois!"

There was no doubt who the crowd wanted to win. They didn't like Indians in general and they didn't like quiet, arrogant breeds like Prine in particular.

Dubois jumped at Prine again.

This time the big man didn't have very good luck. Prine easily dodged the thrust of Dubois's knife. Dubois, off balance, fell to one knee.

The crowd cried out. "Get up, Dubois!" "Kill the breed, Dubois!" "Come on, Dubois!"

Even Barton Jaeger himself had gotten caught up in the excitement. He, too, had cupped his hands and was yelling.

Dubois got to his feet and started circling Prine again.

"Yer gonna regret ever comin' here, breed," Dubois said.

Prine got the next cut in.

He slashed his knife across the front of Dubois's shirt. A line of blood spurted across the cotton material and started soaking the fiber immediately.

Dubois made the mistake of looking down at the wound and for his trouble, he got cut a second time, a long, deep gash along the side of his neck.

"You sonofabitchin' breed," Dubois said.

And put his head down and used himself like a battering ram, hurling himself forward into Prine's chest.

This time Prine wasn't quick enough to get away.

Dubois's head got him right in the solar plexus, knocking the wind out of him and knocking Prine back into the crowd.

Several crowd members tried to grab Prine and take his knife from him but he pulled himself to freedom and went back at Dubois.

Prine started circling again but closer, closer.

Blood was now running from Dubois's neck down into the fabric of his shirt. He was starting to get pretty messy.

Dubois added to his own problems by tripping and starting to fall to his feet.

Prine started to come in at him but a man from the crowd grabbed Prine's shoulder and wouldn't let him go until Dubois had had time to regain his feet.

This time, Prine went directly at Dubois.

He shifted his knife to his left hand, freeing his right hand for battling.

He punched Dubois hard in the mouth. The big man's legs got wobbly.

The crowd cried its protest.

Then he slammed a second blow into Dubois's chest. Dubois started going over backward. Between loss of blood and the hard shot to the mouth, he was starting to crumble.

And then the gunfire sounded.

No matter how intrigued the crowd was with the knife fight, it turned its attention as one to the front of the stockade where a sentry was crying, "I got me a Mountie! I got me a Mountie!"

The man's words were like throwing raw meat to a hungry animal.

The notion of a Mountie being captured at the stockade was great news.

Barton Jaeger joined the crowd running toward the front.

Brother Edmund pulled on his sleeve. "But what about burning the man in the pit and finding the truth?"

Jaeger looked down at him and laughed. "Listen, you crazy old bastard. Right now there are more important things than your superstitions. You understand me?"

Brother Edmund looked devastated.

chapter
sixteen

THE MEN GOT CONSTABLE ABERNATHY UP BY
the campfire. David Adams knelt next to him.

Not until he'd seen the youth wounded—his entire chest
heaving with blood as Abernathy fought for life—had he
realized how frail and young the constable looked.

"How's he doing?" one of the men asked.

All David Adams could do was shake his head.

Hanrahan, whose medical reading had never been more
critical than now, leaned over and said, "We'd better get
the bleeding stopped, sir."

"And you know how to do that?"

"Yessir, I do."

"You're sure?"

"Pretty sure, sir."

David Adams looked at Abernathy's pale, drawn face
one more time, then said, "Why don't you take over then,
Hanrahan?"

"Yessir."

So Hanrahan knelt down and got to work.

"Sir?"

"Yes."

"Somebody coming."

"Where?"

"Other side of the hill."

"How do you know?"

"I hear dogs bark."

"I see. Good observation, Munster."

"Thank you, sir."

Half an hour after Hanrahan started working on Abernathy, David Adams was still nearby.

He'd been drinking coffee and muttering a few silent prayers for Abernathy when recruit Munster called out about the visitor on the other side of the hill.

Now, picking up his Snider and making certain that his long-barreled revolver was properly holstered, Adams rose and went over to see how Abernathy was doing.

Hanrahan, working quickly, glanced up at the sergeant and said, "At least we don't have to worry about him bleeding to death anymore."

"Good work, Hanrahan."

Adams took appreciative note of how well Hanrahan had wound the white gauze and bandages around Abernathy's chest.

"And I got the bullet."

"What?"

"The bullet, sir. I took it out."

Adams was astonished. "You did?"

"Yessir." He grinned, looking like a kid himself. "It's a good thing I read chapter twelve last week, I guess."

"Chapter twelve?"

"That's the chapter on how to get a bullet out."

"I see."

"Very important chapter, wouldn't you say, sir?"

Adams smiled. "Yes, Hanrahan, I'd say that's probably an important chapter."

He nodded good-bye and then left the warmth and glow of the campfire, and headed up the steep grassy hill to where Munster had been calling from.

"Evening, sir."

"Evening."

"If you'll look right down there," Munster said. And raised a white gloved hand and pointed down into the deep shadows at the bottom of the long hill.

"Walking," Munster said.

Adams still hadn't been able to see anybody—

"There, sir."

And then a figure emerged from the darkness and walked into the moonlight.

Adams recognized right away that the person was a woman.

But my God, what would a woman be doing out here at this time, wandering around?

Munster raised his Snider. Drew a bead on her.

"Could be a decoy, sir."

"Decoy?"

"Sure. She could be leading a raiding party."

"I see." Adams tried to keep his amusement from his tone. When he'd been younger, and a constable, he'd been just like Munster here. He'd had a very active imagination. This couldn't possibly be something as simple as a woman who'd lost her way—this had to be a woman who was leading an Indian war party, even though the woman looked white and even though there was no Indian war party to be seen anywhere.

Adams started down the hill.

"Sir?"

He turned back to Munster. "Yes, Constable?"

"I just wanted you to know."

"Know, Munster?"

"Yessir." And here he patted his Snider. "That I've got you covered."

"Ah."

"So there's no reason to be scared."

"Thanks for telling me that, Munster. Now I don't have to take my nerve tonic."

And with that, smiling, Adams went down the hill to meet the woman.

Not until he was halfway there did he realize that the woman was Louise Weller.

"Louise?"

"David?"

He walked even faster now, being careful of the innumerable gopher holes that dotted this land.

"What're you doing out here?"

"My horse," she said. "Broke his leg and I had to—" She shook her head.

"But what're you doing out here in the first place? Is something wrong with Robert?"

As they stood looking at each other in the moonlight, the night wind soft with the scent of pine and spring dirt, she took his elbow and said, "I need to talk to you, David. You're not going to like what you hear. I mean, you're not going to think much of me after I tell you the truth."

"I find that hard to believe, Louise."

She smiled sadly. "Don't be noble till I've finished telling you everything, David. Then if you still want to be noble, I'll appreciate it."

"Is everything all right, sir?" Munster shouted down from the hill.

"Everything's fine," Adams shouted back.

"Just checking, sir."

"Thank you, Constable." Again, he tried to keep the irritation from his voice.

Constable Munster might be overly zealous but it was better to be too much than too little in a territory as rough as this one.

"All right," Adams said, turning back to Louise Weller, "now tell me this shocking story."

She dropped her gaze for a moment and then shook her head. "I haven't been a faithful wife, David. I haven't been faithful at all."

Adams's stomach tightened. He knew now that Louise hadn't been exaggerating.

Her story was indeed going to be shocking.

chapter
seventeen

JAEGER AND DUBOIS LED THE CROWD TO THE front of the stockade, where two of the sentries were dragging a scarlet-coated man into the torchlight.

Seeing this, the crowd got excited. A few months ago a sneak thief had been caught and hanged right here at the stockade—following a "trial" that was pure comic delight to watch—and now the crowd sensed that the man in the scarlet coat might provide the same kind of thrill.

No doubt about it: the thought of stringing up a Mountie sounded mighty good to a lot of people.

The sentries dragged the protesting Mountie into the stockade's central yard and threw him at Jaeger's feet.

"Caught him tryin' to sneak in," one of the sentries said breathlessly, grinning and obviously proud of himself.

"Don't you know who the hell I am?" the Mountie said, looking up at Jaeger.

"Afraid I don't," Jaeger said.

"Hang 'im!" somebody shouted from the back of the crowd.

Prine stepped forward then, looked down at the Mountie, and said, "He's our informant at the fort."

Carmichael looked very grateful to see Prine.

Disappointment spread like a virus across the crowd. Faces that had been grinning now slumped into frowns.

Here they'd had a full evening's entertainment planned and now Prine had gone and spoiled it for them.

Several crowd members looked longingly back at Frank

Adams, who was still tied to the post in the center of the pit.

Maybe later tonight they could get back to him. Hanging a plain lawman wasn't as much fun as hanging a Mountie but you had to take what you got.

"Bring him over to my cabin," Jaeger said to Prine.

Jaeger put his cigar in his face and took off striding toward his cabin.

A few of the little kids dogged his heels. One of them said, "Don't we get to kill him, Mr. Jaeger, huh, don't we?"

Jaeger smiled. "You boys sure seem to have the blood lust now, don't you?"

"Pa says that if we help hang a Mountie, ever'body in the territory will be scairt of us."

"Well, that's true as far as it goes," Jaeger said. "But also remember that if you kill a Mountie, all the other Mounties will come lookin' for you."

Jaeger laughed to himself and strode even faster toward his cabin, glancing around as he walked. At night, bathed in the deep shadows of the torches, the interior of the stockade was almost appealing. During the day, you saw how crude all the buildings were, composed of rough-sawed lumber and scrap metal and newspaper and tar paper. But at night there was a primitive beauty to the place. The only thing that spoiled the effect was the stench. Toilet facilities were hopelessly bad and people had never learned how to carry their garbage down to the river and throw it in.

Jaeger made up his mind to have a general meeting one of these days and talk about cleaning the place up.

Like all leaders who'd ruled for a long time, he had begun to think of the people as his servants. He wanted the stockade to become a fitting tribute to himself. And in its present condition, it was hardly a decent tribute to a man of his stature.

He reached his cabin, opened the door, and went inside.

Anne was careful not to pack more than she could easily carry in a knapsack.

From the bed, in the dark night and in the dark fog of his

liquored-up state, her father said, "What're you doin' over there, anyway?"

"Just looking for something, Pa."

"Lookin' for what?"

"Knitting needle." She hated her ability to lie easily. She didn't want to get into the habit.

"I'm tryin' t'sleep."

"I'm sorry I woke you, Pa."

There was a pause and then he said, "You still mad about what I tole you earlier?"

"No, Pa."

"You sure?"

"Yes, Pa. I'm sure."

"We'll talk about it some more in the morning. But I ain't gonna change my mind."

"I know that, Pa. Now get to sleep."

"This is just the way it's got to be."

"Yes, Pa."

"Night."

"Night, Pa."

There were certain times—certain times when she forgot about the beatings he'd inflicted on her and her mother all her life; when she forgot about the fact that he was drunk nearly all the time—that she felt sorry for her father. As now. Tonight, Dubois had come here and put two hundred dollars in the old man's hand and then asked for Anne's hand in marriage.

Next week the wedding was to be, Dubois had said.

So the old man had obliged him.

Two hundred dollars would keep him in corn liquor for a good long time.

So tonight the old man had given her his final, official word.

She was to marry Dubois. Next week.

Which was why now, in the shadows directly across from Pa's bed, Anne was putting her knapsack together.

She would sneak away tonight. Forever.

She sat on the edge of her bed, doing nothing but staring

into the darkness until she heard the soft, wet snoring sounds Pa always made.

He went to sleep so quickly. Alcohol turned people into infants again, vulnerable and helpless. Pa had wasted his own life on corn liquor.

She listened to all the shouting outside.

From what she'd been able to gather, a Mountie had been caught sneaking up to the stockade.

Recalling the recent lynching, she felt sorry for the man they'd caught tonight.

She had never seen anything uglier than that lynching.

The man had not quite died when they slapped the horse away from under him. The man had taken a long time, just hanging there, to choke to death. His hands kept grasping at his neck. He fouled himself, front and back, terribly. And even when he was dying, people kept jeering him and pelting him with stones. And not just the adults. The children, too, stood beneath the hanging man and shouted dirty words and laughter up at him. One little boy even took a jackknife and aimed it right at the hanging man's crotch and struck it deep in the man's scrotum. The crowd had gone crazy.

Tonight, she knew, might well be a repeat of that. And she didn't want to be around to see it.

Nor did she want to be around when Dubois came looking for his bride next week.

Now that Pa was asleep again, she returned to picking out the few shirts and pants and socks that would fit in her knapsack.

In a few hours, the stockade would quiet down. She would slip out in the darkness.

And hopefully, Prine would go with her.

She had made her mind up to ask him.

She realized that her leaving—especially if she left with Prine—would likely kill Pa but she no longer cared.

She wanted a decent life, and children, and her own homestead and she would never get it if she stayed in the stockade.

She packed, hearing how the chants of the crowd had shifted from the front of the stockade to over by Jaeger's cabin.

She wondered what had happened to the Mountie.
She sure hoped they didn't hang him.

Jaeger had poured himself some bourbon and was just turning back to his desk when the knock came on his front door.

He saw Prine silhouetted against the torches in the yard.

"Come in," Jaeger said, taking a sip of his bourbon and seating himself behind his desk.

A leather chair and mahogany fireplace lent the cabin an air of worldliness. Jaeger did not want to think of himself the way he thought of the others who lived in the stockade—as human garbage. Generation after generation of garbage, he sometimes thought; the kids as scruffy and stupid as the parents.

Someday he would leave the stockade and sail for England where, given all the money he'd managed to squirrel away, he'd live a high-tone life in London. When not living the high-tone life in Paris, that is.

The Mountie who walked through the door was young and scared. Actually, he looked more like a youngster masquerading as a Mountie than he did the real thing.

"Mr. Jaeger?"

"That's me, son," Jaeger said, taking a drag on his cigar.

"My name's Carmichael."

"You were doing a little work for us at the fort?"

"Yessir."

"And you found out what exactly?"

Behind him, Prine closed the door and came into the cabin. Lamplight lent everything a burnished silkiness.

Prine stood a few feet behind Carmichael, listening, silent. It was his silence that drove most white man crazy. It wasn't right for anybody—not even a breed—to be as quiet as Prine was.

"They're on their way here right now, sir."

"I expected they would be, son. After all, we did kidnap Sergeant Adams's brother."

"Yessir."

Jaeger eyed the young man closely. "But you've got

something else to tell me, don't you?"

Carmichael gulped nervously. "Yessir." His voice was scarcely a whisper.

"But something's stopping you, isn't it?"

"Yessir."

"Are you afraid to tell me?"

"No, sir."

"Is somebody stopping you from telling me?"

"No, sir."

"Then what is it?"

Carmichael, looking awfully fancy in his scarlet coat and Stetson, dropped his eyes.

"He wants more money," Prine said.

And Jaeger smiled. "So that's it?"

"Yessir."

"You've come across a piece of information you think I should know but you want more money for it. Is that right?"

"Pretty much, sir."

"This must be some hot piece of information."

"Yessir, I think it is."

"How much would you say it's worth?"

"Well, now, sir, I—"

"Don't be shy, son. Speak up."

Carmichael named a price.

Prine laughed. Jaeger just looked at him.

"You don't have very modest goals, do you, son?"

"No, sir, I guess I don't."

"And you really think this piece of information is worth it?"

"Yessir, I do."

Jaeger opened the middle drawer in his desk. He took a packet of currency from the drawer and tossed the currency in the center of the desk.

"That's a lot of money, son."

"It certainly is, sir."

"And it's yours if I think your information's good enough. Is that fair?"

"Very fair, sir."

"All right, then. Give me the information."

"Yessir."

So Carmichael told Jaeger all about how the Indians planned to sneak David Adams into the stockade where he would free his brother and escape.

"Anne?"

She was right at the front door of the cabin when he woke up abruptly and called her name.

"Yes?"

"Where you going so late?"

"Just for a walk."

"Not to see that goddamn breed, are you?"

"No, Father, not to see Prine."

"You be back right away. You know how I get some-times."

He woke disoriented from the corn liquor occasionally and then got scared when he couldn't figure out where he was. She had to come and sit on the edge of the bed and hold his hand till he felt better.

"I won't be long, Father."

"You promise?"

"I promise."

She leaned forward, about to put her hand on the doorknob.

Once outside, she'd hurry to Prine's wigwam and convince him to run off with her.

By dawn, they'd be on their way to a new life.

But a curious guilt came over her.

Terrible as he'd been to her, she'd miss her father in certain ways.

She looked back through the gloom, to where she could hear him wheezing on the bed.

Good-bye, old man, she said to herself.

I don't wish you a terrible life. I really don't.

And then she grabbed the doorknob, gave it a turn, and started out into the night.

The cool breeze of evening balmed. She felt free already as she stepped down the stairs to the hard-packed earth, her knapsack stuffed to overflowing.

She hurried to the back of the stockade, where she'd make her way through the shadows to Prine's wigwam.

Reaching Prine's took nearly ten minutes.

Once, she was certain that the sentry had seen her. She stopped in her tracks, closing her eyes and clenching her fists and holding her breath, as if she were trying to will herself to be invisible.

But then he'd passed on and she continued her flight to the wigwam.

When she reached it, Anne made sure that no eyes were watching her, she opened the entrance flap and looked inside.

Only darkness greeted her.

Prine was not here.

To her right, then, she heard human feet roughly trampling twigs.

It could be Prine, in which case she'd be perfectly safe.

But what if it wasn't Prine?

What if it were one of the sentries?

Frightened now, she hastened inside the wigwam, letting the flap fall closed behind her.

The darkness smelled of Prine's pipe.

She huddled next to the pole that held the wigwam aloft.

Outside, the feet drew nearer, nearer.

Please God, she thought. Please let it be Prine. And please help him to see that running away with me is the best thing for both of us.

Closer came the sound of snapping twigs.

Somebody was approaching the wigwam now.

The flap was thrown back.

She saw a male torso in the flapway.

She could not see the head.

But somehow she didn't think this was Prine.

Why would he pause so long before coming inside?

She wanted to hide in the corner but she knew it was no use. Prine's wigwam was bare and offered no place to hide at all.

The man bent down and peered inside.

The voice told her immediately who it was.

"You little whore, I should have known I'd find you here."

Dubois drew his knife from his belt and proceeded into the wigwam.

"You little whore," he said again.

chapter
eighteen

DAVID ADAMS LISTENED TO LOUISE WELLER'S
story with great sorrow.

They leaned against a granite boulder, David puffing on
his pipe and looking up at the moon in the soft night.

"He doesn't have much of a life left already, and look
what I've done to him, David."

"Don't be foolish, Louise."

But she went on with her bitter reverie. "I even told myself
that I shouldn't feel guilty, that the way Robert treated me
justified what I was doing."

"It hasn't been easy for you, Louise. The accident changed
Robert. There's no doubt about that."

"It hasn't been easy for Robert, either."

David smoked his pipe, looked now at the campfire near
the copse of birches beneath them.

"You haven't told him?"

"No. It would destroy him."

"But he suspects," David said.

"He knows I've gone somewhere a few nights. That's
all."

"He's suggested you're meeting someone else?"

"Suggested it, yes. But that's different from knowing
anything."

David exhaled pipe tobacco. He loved the sweet taste of
the smoke in his mouth. "You could always tell him."

"Oh, God, David, I couldn't. I really couldn't."

"And you could always move into a city—the two of you,
I mean—and start over. There would be work for him in the
city. Out here he's just rotting."

"But he loves the land so much."

"He can always take trips to the country. But I'd sure try and steer him toward some kind of constructive job. Sitting in a wheelchair all day and watching you do farm chores won't help his self-respect much."

She leaned into him and touched his arm. "Well, at least I'll get something from my time with Jaeger."

"And what would that be?"

She looked up at him. "He's in love with me."

"I see."

"And that means I can influence him."

He stared at her, taking the last drags of the tobacco bowl.

"What if you're wrong?"

"Wrong?"

"What if you get in the stockade and Jaeger decides not to let either one of you go?"

"I don't think that will happen."

"But you're not sure."

"No, not positive of course but—"

He leaned over and took her shoulders. "You're confused about things right now, Louise. So I think you'd better let me handle things my way."

"You think you can get your brother out?"

"I think so."

And he told her the plan he'd concocted with the Indians to get inside the stockade.

"You think it'll work, David?"

"It's about our only hope. We're pretty badly outnumbered otherwise."

"I'll say a prayer for you." She frowned. "If you don't mind having somebody like me saying prayers, that is."

"There's nothing wrong with you, Louise. You made a mistake."

"A terrible one."

"Well, it's a terrible time in your life and so maybe a terrible mistake is inevitable."

"You really think we should move to a city?"

"I really do."

"Will you help me convince Robert of that?"

He slid his arm around her shoulder and started walking her back toward the campfire.

"I'll be glad to help you, Louise. Glad to."

Dubois came into the darkened wigwam, his knife glinting in the moonlight. "You little whore.

"What're you doing here?"

"It's none of your business," Anne said.

"You don't seem to remember. You're going to marry me."

"No, Dubois, you're wrong. I'll never marry you no matter what happens."

Dubois received those words the way he received most of Anne's words—with a dull ache that would result ultimately in anger.

Dubois had never loved a woman before. To Dubois, most women were to be used for pleasure and then discarded.

But Anne Fallon was different. Much as he prided himself on strength, she made him weak. Much as he prided himself on common sense, she made him foolish.

Many nights he lay in his lean-to, listening to rain pelt the stretched buffalo hide wall, and he thought of Anne.

Kind thoughts of Anne. Pleasant thoughts of Anne.

He looked at her now in the darkness, little more than a shadow that talked at the present moment, and he felt that terrible longing ache he'd known for well over a year.

He wanted to touch her gently, and be touched gently in return.

He wanted to say kind, soft words to her, and receive kind, soft words in return.

"Anne."

The sweetness of his own voice startled him.

"What?"

"I want to be your friend."

"You come in with a knife and say that?"

"I'll put the knife away."

"You kill people, Dubois. I could never love anybody who did that."

"I'll change."

"It's too late for you, Dubois." She paused then. "Dubois, don't you see that this can't work?"

"We need to give it a chance."

"No matter how much of a chance we give it, it won't work. I—I'm sorry."

Anne had been curiously touched by Dubois's softer tone. Now, she softened her own voice. She realized for the first time that beneath the shaggy, filthy, violent being who was Dubois there dwelt a human being.

"Anne?"

"Yes?"

"We could get a homestead."

"Please, Dubois. Don't make this any more difficult for either of us."

For a time he said nothing. Just listened to the wind in the trees.

"Anne?"

"Dubois, please just let me walk out of here right now."

"A man can change."

"No, Dubois, a man can't change that much."

"I only kill people when I get mad. That don't mean I'm bad."

"Please, Dubois. Just let me walk out of here."

She took a first tentative step toward the front of the wigwam.

He moved to block her.

For a wonderful moment she'd felt that she'd be able to walk past Dubois.

For a wonderful moment she wondered if she hadn't been wrong about him, if he might not be a lot more civilized than she'd thought.

But now she knew.

Dubois was Dubois.

Violent, vile.

He said, "I won't let that breed have you."

"He's a good man, Dubois, whether you think so or not."

"He's a breed."

"He's also kind and gentle to me."

Dubois shook his head. The notion of Prine putting his hands on Anne profoundly sickened him.

"You shouldn't be with him."

"That's for me to decide."

She took another step.

"Please let me go, Dubois."

He said nothing.

She took one more step.

She was much nearer the entrance now. Behind Dubois she could see the night sky.

Freedom had never seemed as sweet to her. She wanted to be outside, to walk where she wished, to feel the night breeze and hear the night song of birds.

Dubois watched her come near him.

The sickness in his stomach was greater than ever.

He saw now, in some final way, that she indeed wanted nothing to do with him, that she indeed loved the half-breed Prine.

She would never be his. Never.

His hand lashed out and grabbed her by the wrist.

"Please, Dubois, you're hurting me."

He slapped her hard across the mouth.

The sound of the slap echoed inside the wigwam.

She started to scream but Dubois clamped his hand across her mouth and then threw her down to the dark floor.

At first, he was hardly aware of what he was doing.

Keeping his hand pasted firmly over her mouth, he wrestled around on the dark floor with her.

Only gradually did he become aware that his free hand was beginning to rip away her clothes.

She kicked and punched him but she didn't slow him down at all.

The more they wrestled, the more he tore at her clothes, the more he felt a great, dark lust for her.

If he couldn't have her the way he wanted her, then he'd have her any way he could.

She bit the palm of his hand pressed to her mouth.

He wanted to cry out but he knew he didn't want to bring others running.

He swallowed down his pain, feeling warm blood oozing from the palm.

As if in retaliation, he ripped away the entire front of her dress.

With his free hand he reached up and touched her warm, perfectly shaped breasts.

She slapped him hard on the side of the head but he kept feeling her breasts. His lust was growing intolerable now.

He tore away the last of her dress.

She was left virtually naked and as he pressed against her, he felt the luxurious heat of her sex.

He struggled to pull his trousers down.

She fought him all the way with a series of slaps and elbows and knees.

But he would not be dissuaded. Not now.

When he put himself into her, he had to hold his hand down tighter than ever on her mouth. He could hear her screaming crazily, the sound dying in her throat and mouth.

For Anne, all this was still the worst kind of nightmare. She'd come over to the wigwam looking for Prine. They would run away together and be free.

Instead, she was now on the floor and Dubois was pushing himself inside her.

It was obvious that she was a virgin but Dubois seemed neither to notice nor care.

He didn't even care about the physical pain he was causing, or the blood that had started to flow from her.

He just kept working away inside her as if she were some tavern whore he'd paid five dollars for the night.

And she kept screaming.

By now her mouth and throat were dry but the sound kept welling up inside her only to be swallowed back down again.

All she could think of was that Prine would someday make things right with Dubois.

"You ain't gonna let that breed have you," Dubois said just after he'd satisfied himself and was pulling out of her. "I promise you that."

And then she saw that all this had taken the most unlikely turn of all.

Not only had Dubois trapped her in the wigwam and raped her. He was now waving his knife as if he were going to kill her.

"No breed's gonna get you, Anne, 'specially not that one."

Gone was the "new" Dubois, the one who'd revealed himself to be warm and caring.

Here was the old Dubois—the real Dubois—the filthy, violent mountain man who was filled with hatred and rage.

But now, given what he'd just done to her, she felt just as filthy as Dubois himself.

She just wanted to be out of here, her knapsack over her shoulder, running down a long moonlight trail to freedom.

She put up one last battle, another round of pushing, scratching, kneeing, and slapping.

But this time Dubois only laughed.

He'd come to see some dark humor in all this. He'd done something the breed had probably wanted to do all this time—he'd partaken of young Anne Fallon's beautiful flesh.

And now here she was trying to push her way free.

Well, he had news for her: She was never going to be free.

Not ever again.

And with that Dubois leaned forward and pressed the cold, sharp blade of the knife to her throat and—

—she knew she was dying the moment she felt the blood on her skin.

She tried to cry out but again it was no use.

He wouldn't take his hand from her mouth.

And with the other hand, he started slicing the knife across her throat.

She soon slipped into unconsciousness, her last real awareness being that the slash across her throat was spurting blood.

There was incredible pain and then—

She felt as if she were being sucked down into a whirlpool, deeper, deeper.

She could feel, smell, and see Dubois above her but then—

—nothing.

She put up a spirited fight and a spirited fuss but then Dubois felt her go limp beneath him—the struggle in her all over now—and he knew she was dead.

He jumped up, pulling his trousers up as he did so.

He wasn't done and he had to hurry.

Killing her was merely the first part of his plan.

The second part was much more sly and would give him just as much satisfaction as raping her had.

He was going to leave her throat-slashed body right where it was, right here in the half-breed's wigwam, and guess who was going to get blamed for killing her?

He hurried from the wigwam, rushing through the trees to the creek where he washed the blood off his hands and arms.

After a while, he realized how he could blame Prine for all this.

chapter
nineteen

BEFORE LEAVING CAMP, ADAMS AND QUANTO
went through their plans one more time.

Simple enough: Quanto and his Indian friends would ride
to the front of the stockade and begin firing rifle shots into
the air. Jaeger and his people would automatically rush out
to see what was going on. While they were all distracted,
Adams would sneak in the rear of the fort, find his brother
and free him.

Once Frank was free, David could then afford to open
fire on the stockade.

As he walked over to his horse, Louise Weller came up.
"I wish you'd think it over, David. Jaeger will listen to me.
He might just let your brother go. I hate to see you take a
risk like this."

"I'll be fine, Louise."

She touched his sleeve. "I'm going to make things right
with Robert. I promise."

He smiled. "I know you will, Louise. You're too good a
woman not to."

Quanto came over. In his right hand he carried a carbine,
in his left a revolver. He stood and looked at Adams and
the woman, saying nothing.

"Well, Louise, we'd better be going."

She nodded, standing there and watching as Adams and
the Indians mounted their horses.

A few minutes later they set off for the stockade.

Prine left Jaeger's cabin a few minutes after ten.

By now, the stockade yard was empty except for a few

stragglers from Brother Edmund's group. They spent most of the night roaming the stockade, muttering prayers to themselves, and looking for further evidence of sin.

There were two of them tonight, dressed as always in the coarse robes of their sect. When they saw Prine, they sneered. In the best traditions of frontier Christianity, they despised anybody who was non-white.

Prine was about halfway across the stockade yard when he heard the shout.

The two fanatics turned to the shout as well.

From across the yard a third fanatic came running, tripping in his robe as he moved.

He held up his hands in the moonlight. Prine could see that they were covered with something glistening and dark.

He knew immediately that he was looking at blood.

When the third fanatic saw Prine, he made a wide arc around the breed and hurried on to his cohorts. The shocked way the fanatic looked at him, Prine might have been a plague carrier.

Ducking down together so that Prine could not hear, the three fanatics whispered frantically to one another.

Prine kept walking toward his wigwam.

And then he heard flapping naked feet behind him.

The fanatics ran up and did their best to encircle him.

"Don't go any farther, breed," said the third fanatic.

Prine, disliking the men more than ever, started to push his way through them and go on back to his wigwam.

But then the fanatics began shouting and it was not long before you could hear people begin to stir in their cabins and tents and lean-tos.

Prine set off walking again but behind him he heard a white voice say, "Stay right where you are, breed."

A grizzled and sleep-rumpled old man with a revolver came around to the front of Prine and joined with the fanatics.

"What'd he do?"

The third fanatic was still breathless from all his running. "Terrible."

"What the hell you talkin' about?" the old man said.

"Prine's wigwam," the third fanatic said, still trying to catch his breath.

"Anne Fallon," one of the other fanatics said. "Prine here murdered her."

"Butchered her is more like it," the third fanatic said, getting his breath back. "You should see what he did to her."

Prine stood still, taking the news without any visible shock.

But already his stomach was knotting up and his heart was hammering wildly in his chest and his body was sleek with a coating of sudden, cold sweat.

He felt so many things. Much as he'd not wanted to admit it, he'd grown attached to the Fallon girl. He wasn't sure he "loved" her—whatever that meant—but he did care for her and care for her deeply. So her death genuinely saddened him.

But her death also frightened him. Everybody in the stockade knew that they had spent time together, and knew of their growing bond. And if she was murdered . . . well, there could be only one logical candidate.

People started drifting into the yard now, rubbing sleep from their faces, hacking up phlegm, pulling up suspenders, tugging on boots.

Soon enough, half of the stockade or better stood in the yard, listening to the fanatic tell his story about how he'd found the Fallon girl savagely murdered in Prine's wigwam.

Not long after, Jaeger appeared.

"What's going on here?" Jaeger said.

The fanatic told him.

Jaeger looked stunned. "You people wait here. I'm going over to Prine's wigwam."

He took a torch from one of the men and set off.

On his way over, he passed by Dubois's small cabin. The man was just coming outside now, tugging on a shirt. He looked as if he'd been enjoying a deep sleep.

"What's all the noise?"

"The Fallon girl."

"What about her?"

"Murdered."

"What the hell're you talking about?"

But Jaeger said nothing, just kept walking grimly toward Prine's wigwam.

Dubois fell into step with him.

The wigwam was dark. Jaeger threw back the flap and pushed the torch inside.

As a boy, Jaeger had seen the aftermath of a massacre some Indians had visited on a white settlement.

The women had looked like this, cut and disfigured and bloody beyond recognition.

Jaeger was afraid he was going to vomit, which would not look good for the leader of the stockade who was supposed to be stronger than the others.

He withdrew his head from the wigwam and stood outside, taking deep breaths of the clean night air.

Dubois took the torch from him and went inside.

Jaeger heard Dubois swearing.

After a minute or so, Dubois came back outside. "The goddamn breed did this, didn't he?"

"It appears so."

"The sonofabitch. Anybody tell her pa?"

"Not yet."

"I'll tell him."

Jaeger smiled faintly. "I'll let you have that honor."

Dubois, his shoulder-length black hair wilder than ever, said, "And then I'm going to take care of the breed myself."

"No," Jaeger said. "We'll call a council. They'll decide."

Dubois started to protest but Jaeger held up his hand. "That's the rule and you know it, Dubois."

"The sonofabitch."

"I know how you feel."

"Goddamn breeds. They should all be killed anyway, just on general principles."

The two men went back to the yard.

The crowd had grown. There was now so much torchlight that the whole yard was lit up.

Carmichael, the turncoat Mountie, was now dressed in

civilian clothes and sitting on Jaeger's stoop. Carmichael had a cigarette going.

"They should be here anytime," Carmichael said.

Jaeger nodded. "Don't worry. I'll be ready for them."

Jaeger went inside the cabin and took down his Remington repeater from its place above the fireplace mantel. He also grabbed a Bible from one of the desk drawers.

He needed both these things to preside over a meeting of the stockade council. He sighed, thinking it was going to be a long night, and thinking also how much he'd like to see Louise Weller tonight.

He still had a raw craving for her both emotionally and sexually. And he had no idea what to do about it.

chapter
twenty

AFTER DAVID ADAMS LEFT CAMP, LOUISE WELLER
decided to stay for a time and see if he returned with his
brother.

While she waited, somewhat shy of the young Mounties
who'd been left in David's wake, she sat on a log sipping
a cup of coffee she'd been offered.

Across from her, painted golden with flames, lay the
wounded Mountie.

Every few minutes the young man would turn slightly in
his sleep and groan with pain.

Having been a nurse for a brief time back in Australia,
Louise decided to put her waiting time to good use and
examine the young man.

She went over and sat next to him.

He was a fine-looking youth, one who reminded her
again of how lonely she felt sometimes without a child to
care for.

She leaned over and examined his bandages. Somebody
had done a good job. They were wrapped well and set in such
a way to both protect the wound and absorb the poisons that
were secreted out.

"How'd I do, ma'am?"

Above her stood a tall youth in a Mountie jacket. He
looked both curious and slightly afraid of what her response
might be.

"You did this?"

"Yes'm."

"Did you ever have any medical training?"

"No, ma'am. Just read a book on the subject when I didn't have nothing else to do in the barracks."

She smiled. "If you keep reading, you might wind up being a doctor."

"I done well?"

"Very well."

"You seem to know what you're talkin' about."

"I was a nurse for four years in Melbourne."

"Australia?"

"Yes."

"Always wanted to go there." He nodded to the fallen Mountie. "How's he doing?"

"He's resting nicely."

"Think he'll make it?"

"Only God knows the answer to that one."

The Mountie stared at his fallen compatriot. "He's kind of an odd duck. Keeps to himself."

"He's a nice-looking boy."

"Too nice-looking some might say. Kind of too well mannered sometimes. Most of us—well, most of us are farm boys from back in the States or one of the provinces up here. Our manners ain't that good."

"So he makes you uncomfortable?"

"Guess that's a pretty good way of puttin' it, ma'am."

Her eyes rested on the sleeping man. Yes, he looked to be the sort who'd make a mother proud. He had a fine good forehead and a fine good nose and a fine strong jaw. She reached out and touched his hand tenderly. "I'm sure if you got to know him, you'd like him."

"Yes, ma'am. I reckon so."

And then the Mountie went back to his friends, who were out in the moonlight tending to their horses.

The wounded man said something.

She wasn't sure what the words were exactly but when she turned back to him, she found his blue eyes open and staring up at her.

"You're not my mother."

She smiled. "No, I'm not."

"Am I dreaming?"

"I don't think so because if you are, then I'm just a figment of your imagination."

"Who are you?"

"My name's Louise."

"I've been shot."

"Yes."

"Am I going to die?"

She saw how frail he was in the firelight, and how eager he looked to hear good news, and so she said, "Oh, no; no, you'll be fine."

"Truly?"

"Truly."

He closed his eyes momentarily. "This really is like a dream."

"I know."

He opened his eyes. "They don't know the truth about me."

"Who?"

"The Mounties."

"I see."

"Abernathy isn't really my name at all."

"It isn't?"

"No. And I lied about where I came from, too."

"Oh?"

"I'm actually a prince." He looked at her and laughed softly. "Can you imagine a crown on my head?"

She studied him a moment. "Yes; yes, I can. And in fine long robes, too."

"You're from England?"

"Australia. But our newspapers were filled with stories and photographs of the English royal family. I never missed a word of it."

He closed his eyes again. "Know why I joined the Mounties?"

"Why?"

"So I could learn to be a man. I don't want to be a spoiled bully like my older brother Edward."

"And have you become a man?"

"No, but I'm a lot closer than I was two years ago when I spent most of my time in the castle letting servants wait on me." He sighed, gulped. He was becoming weak again. "Thank you for listening to me."

"My privilege."

"You seem so nice."

"Well, I hope I'm nice, anyway."

"Will you keep our secret?"

"Of course."

"I just had to tell somebody in case—well, in case I didn't make it."

"I know."

"In my saddlebag you'll find the name of my father in England. Would you contact him?"

"Yes. But I won't be needing to since you'll be fine."

"You really think so?"

"I really think so. And I used to be a nurse."

When she told him that, young Abernathy looked positively happy.

He closed his eyes again, and slept.

It was a testament to Fallon's drinking habits that none of the commotion in the stockade had awakened him.

Dubois tried knocking first but that didn't help, either.

Finally, he jerked the cabin door back, ducked his head, and went inside.

The place smelled of corn liquor, sweat, and sleep.

Somewhere in the darkness toward the back, he could hear the old man snoring violently.

Torchlight from the yard flicked dancing shadows across the cabin walls.

Dubois went back to the old man.

He hated the old sot and he was going to take pleasure in seeing the bastard go crazy over the death of his daughter.

The first thing he did was shake the old man. The second was shout in his face.

The third—and he enjoyed this, too—was take the basin of water from the kitchen table and splash it over the old man's face.

The bastard came up struggling and shouting, as if he were drowning.

He was completely confused and totally frightened.

"Get up, Fallon."

"Wha—what's goin' on?"

"It's Anne."

"What about her?" Badly as the old sot had treated her, it was obvious that in his crude way he'd cared for her, too. There was panic in his voice now, and deep fear.

In the shadows, the old sot looked even older, beard stubble blackening his jaw and cheeks, his white hair fluffy and wild around his head.

"What happened to her?"

"Stabbed."

"Oh, God."

"I didn't want t'tell you but somebody had to."

"Who killed her?"

"The breed."

"Oh, shit. I told her not to hang around him."

"He's in the yard now. We're gonna hang him."

"Oh, God," the old sot said, and started making a noise that was half barking and half sobbing.

He got up from the bed, rubbing his face and shaking his head over and over again.

"Thought you'd want to see the trial."

"You're a good friend, Dubois. I appreciate it."

Dubois's mind was filled with images of Anne Fallon dying there on the floor of the wigwam.

They went out into the yard.

There were enough torches now that the place glowed like daylight. Even the children were up and ringed around the center of the yard where Jaeger sat behind a table with a gavel at one hand and his Bible at the other. On top of the Bible sat his pistol. If God didn't bring justice, then Jaeger was determined to. Jaeger kept thinking about the Mounties sneaking in the rear of the stockade but he'd posted a sentry there to warn everybody.

Now, the breed stood in crude shackles before Jaeger. People pelted him with spittle and rocks.

The breed's head hung down. Blood poured from a gash on his right cheek. A six-year-old girl had gotten him good by throwing a jagged piece of glass at him.

Jaeger said, "Several people here have testified that they found the Fallon girl in your wigwam. What do you have to say to that?"

The breed kept his head down, said nothing.

"Here is your chance to defend yourself," Jaeger said. There was a note of something like sympathy in his voice. Obviously he wanted the breed to at least go through the motions of defending himself.

But the breed said nothing.

Dubois brought the old man to the edge of the crowd. Jaeger looked up and saw him.

"You know anything about this, Fallon?" Jaeger said.

"Only that I tole her not to hang around this here breed, that no good'd come of it."

"You're the one who found her, Dubois. You have anything to say?"

"Just that I know he killed her."

"You know that for sure? You saw him kill her?"

Dubois faltered a moment. "Not saw her. But I know it."

"And we know it, too!" somebody shouted from the crowd.

You could see they were all ready for a hanging. In a stockade such as this one, where law was crude at best and real justice was a seldom thing, hanging was one of the main social events. It served to remind people that even among thieves there had to be a modicum of honesty, and that even the roughest of men could be called to task for their behavior.

Jaeger saw this now, too.

It would be a good thing to let this mob at the breed. They had long hated him. And Jaeger could prove to them that he was one of them by handing the breed over.

He sat forward and looked at Prine now.

"If you have anything to say for yourself, breed, you'd better say it now, otherwise you won't be getting any more chances."

The breed looked up at him and then deftly sent a silver missile of spittle across the desk and right next to Jaeger's folded hands.

Jaeger shook his head. "I'd say it's time we hung this breed—what d'you folks think?"

The crowd cheered their agreement.

Corporal McKenzie stood on the crest of a hill near the Mountie camp listening to the sudden ruckus.

Earlier, he'd heard gunfire. Now it was cheering.

He wondered what was going on there.

He had the feeling he should gather the patrol and ride over to the stockade but Sergeant Adams had told him to stay put, that sight of the Mounties would only incite the stockade people, which is why he'd used the Indians rather than the Mounties as decoys.

The stockade people would merely fire at the Indians— the Mounties they would pursue and the bloodshed would be terrible.

Corporal McKenzie stood drawing on his pipe, listening to the distant ruckus.

He was a man of action. Simply standing by like this was very frustrating to him.

Frank Adams watched the "trial" from his place at the post. They were going to hang the breed. There was no doubt about that. None at all.

Two burly men stepped in now and grabbed the breed by either arm and then they started dragging him across the yard.

Women and children started hurling stones at the breed again. Some of them landed so hard, you could hear the bones crunch.

The mob was headed just one place, to an almost grotesquely big oak tree that rested at the west end of the yard.

Here a horse sat waiting. And so did a rope, one end tossed over a thick branch, the other tied neatly into a hangman's noose.

Frank strained at his bonds but he knew he'd never get free.

He watched as Jaeger worked his way free from the mob and walked over to the pit.

"Enjoying the festivities?"

"There's nothing like a good lynching," Frank said.

"I'm glad you think that way because you'll be next." The smirk vanished from Jaeger's face and voice. "My brother isn't a strong man."

"He was strong enough to kill somebody."

But Jaeger seemed not to hear.

"I know what they do to men who aren't strong. The convicts never leave them alone."

"Maybe your brother should have thought about that before he fired that gun."

Jaeger smiled again. "But there's one pleasure I can take, Adams. Someday my brother will be getting out of prison but you'll never be getting out of your grave."

A cheer went up from the crowd. The men had thrown the breed up on the horse.

"They'll be all primed up by the time they get to you. The little kids'll probably give you a concussion with their rocks before the noose snaps your neck."

"If you're tryin' to scare me, Jaeger, you're not."

"Oh? You're not afraid to die?"

"Oh, I'm afraid to die, all right, but I'm just not sure that this mob of riffraff is smart enough to know how to hang a man."

Jaeger laughed bitterly. "I'll pass along your sentiments."

Jaeger turned back to the crowd now and watched.

The rope that came down from the massive branch was cinched around the breed's neck.

Another cheer went up.

Then some more stones were thrown at the breed. Frank could see the man jump and jerk as the heavy rocks landed brutally on his torso and face. These women and children had a real taste for violence, no doubt about that.

"Hang 'im!" somebody shouted.

And then it became a chant that the whole crowd took up.

And then they hung him.

No matter how slow the buildup might be, the actual hanging was always fast.

The crowd had parted just enough so Frank could see the man slap the horse's rump and the horse jump ahead, leaving the breed there dangling.

Whoever had done the knot had done a good job because Frank could see the breed's neck snap. It was a clean snap and in that respect the breed had been lucky. Frank had seen a man in Nevada spend nearly twenty minutes flailing around on the end of a rope. Even the bloodthirstiest men of the mob had had misgivings about that one. The man was pretty much a mess by the time death finally took him.

The breed swung under the branch now.

The women and children resumed their rock throwing.

Their stones slammed into him so hard that his body seemed to dance around.

One kid got the breed a good strong one right in the nose—smashing the bone—and the breed started bleeding as if he were leaking.

Frank looked away.

Jaeger was right there smiling.

"Don't forget, lawman. You're next."

Then Jaeger went over to join the crowd in the festivities. Several jugs of corn liquor were being passed around.

chapter
twenty-one

QUANTO AND THE OTHER INDIANS RODE DOWN the steep, grassy hill behind Sergeant David Adams.

The stockade was now in sight and David was going over the plan one last time.

Quanto and his men would ride close to the fort and begin whooping and shooting.

The people in the stockade would rush toward the front and begin returning the fire.

While they were distracted, David Adams would sneak in the rear of the stockade and look for his brother.

Adams held up his white-gloved hand to get the Indians to stop.

"Do you have any questions?"

Quanto shook his head. He said something to his braves in their native tongue. The Indians shook their heads.

"Let me go first then," Adams said. "Give me a little time to work my way around back and then start firing. Do you understand?"

Quanto nodded.

Adams gave a half salute of good-bye and then took off down the hill.

She sat by the campfire, watching the moon start to travel down behind the hill.

Nearby, Abernathy slept while the other Mounties settled in.

One, somewhere behind the copse of trees to her right, walked sentry.

She kept thinking of David Adams. Louise and her husband certainly had no better friend.

And she knew that David was on an impossible mission. Barton Jaeger was many things—good and bad alike, actually—but one thing he was not was forgiving. The times he'd talked to her about his brother, she'd heard pure rage in his voice. He was afraid that his brother would somehow be killed while he was in prison. The thought of this made him seem crazy from time to time.

She could not imagine that he would let either Frank Adams or his brother David live under any circumstances.

And David was walking right into Jaeger's clutches.

"Ma'am?"

She turned and saw Abernathy staring up at her.

"Hello," she said.

"I was wondering if I could have a drink of water." His wound had dehydrated him. His voice was raspy.

"Of course."

She went over to where a canteen was kept. She brought it back and put it to his lips.

She could see the satisfaction in his eyes.

"Tastes good."

"Good."

"Ma'am?"

"Yes."

"Is it all right if I say something?"

"Of course."

"Even if it isn't any of my business?"

She smiled. "What is it you'd like to say?"

"You look troubled."

She nodded. "I suppose I do."

"You've got something troubling you."

She sighed. "Many things troubling me, actually."

"Any way I can help? You've certainly helped me."

"I wish there were."

She thought of her husband Robert, wondering what he'd be doing now. He'd been such a strapping, happy man before the accident.

But after—

She wanted to hold him as she once had, be all the things she'd been to him, wife, lover, soul mate. But she wondered if that would ever be possible again.

"A princess cries tears of pure silver."

The words snatched her from her reverie. "Pardon me?"

" 'A princess cries tears of pure silver.' My father always used to say that to my sister whenever she cried." He looked into her face. "You look as if you're about to cry."

"I suppose I do."

"I wouldn't mind. I mean, it wouldn't embarrass me."

She laughed. "Well, maybe sometime I'll take you up on that offer."

She stood up, walked over by the trees, looked out on the great plains.

David was out there somewhere, headed for the stockade.

She should have gone with him. If she were truly his friend, that's just what she would have done.

And then she thought: Why not?

Why don't I get on a horse right now and ride to the stockade myself?

Jaeger will listen to me. I know he will.

She turned hastily back to the campfire.

Abernathy lay there watching her gather her things.

"You're going someplace?"

"To help your Sergeant Adams."

"You could get hurt."

She smiled down at him. "So could he and that's just what I'm afraid of."

Without asking permission, she went down to where the horses were feeding, mounted one, and rode off as several Mounties shouted in the night behind her.

chapter
twenty-two

DAVID ADAMS HAD JUST REACHED THE REAR OF the stockade when he heard the gunfire up near the front.

Quanto and his friends had done just what they'd said they would.

Adams had been surprised by the number of people milling around in the yard of the stockade. Some kind of event had just taken place, though Adams wasn't sure what it was. Most of the stockade seemed to be awake despite the late hour. This would just make Adams's task all the more difficult.

The first reaction to Quanto's gunfire was confusion.

Parents hurried children back to their various shelters. Babies cried; mothers shouted for children they couldn't find.

Quanto and his friends kept up the gunfire.

All of the torches were quickly extinguished. The stockade lay in moonlight and deep shadow as the men of the stockade manned the flour bags and timber and rock that formed the stockade's front wall. These men were already returning the gunfire.

At the rear of the place, David Adams belly-crawled underneath a crude timber fence.

From here, he could see the layout of the stockade, how everything was set on the edges of the wide, circular yard, and how the retaining wall at the front of the place had been set up to keep strangers out.

"Stop right there."

David Adams froze.

Even above the gunfire, he could clearly hear the sharp command of the sentry.

Because of all the noise at the front of the place, David hadn't heard the sentry sneak up.

Now the young man stood over him, carbine at the ready.

"You just drop that rifle," the sentry said.

And so David did, laying his Snider down carefully.

"Push it out away from you."

Which is just what David did also.

But as he was doing so, his right leg lashed out, quickly entwining itself around the left calf of the sentry, pulling the man down hard to the ground.

Before the sentry's head had even contacted the grass, David was hitting him hard in the temple, knocking him out immediately.

Chest heaving, body covered in sweat, David knelt there listening to his heart hammering and to the warlike sounds ahead of him.

He hoped Quanto and his men were all right.

He hadn't meant for them to die.

The gunfire continued uninterrupted.

David Adams got back down on his belly and crawled the rest of the way into the stockade.

Louise Weller found a timber trail and stuck to it.

She wondered if Jaeger had discovered David yet.

She rode faster, faster toward the stockade.

By the time Abernathy cried out, all the other Mounties were sitting around the campfire. Except for the sentry, of course.

McKenzie looked over and took in the situation immediately.

In his sleep, Abernathy had rolled over on his stomach and had thereby inflicted great pain on himself.

Now, he didn't have the strength to roll over so that he once more rested on his back.

McKenzie threw off his blanket, jumped to his stockinged

feet, and went over to help his fallen comrade.

The other men slept soundly, snoring and whispering in their dreams.

Abernathy was soaked with his own sweat and blood.

McKenzie got him back into proper position and then got Hanrahan to change the dressing on the wound.

As Hanrahan worked to make Abernathy comfortable, he allowed his mind to think about how proud his father would be of him at the moment. Maybe the Hanrahan family had not produced an official doctor yet, but they had produced at least one son who knew something of medicine.

His fingers worked quickly, deftly.

Soon enough Abernathy quit groaning in pain, though Hanrahan could see by the other man's eyes that he was in delirium.

"Just don't tell anybody that I'm a lord, will you, Mrs. Weller? They'd never let me live it down."

So Abernathy thought that Hanrahan was Mrs. Weller.

Hanrahan took a clean piece of cloth and wiped the sweat and grime from Abernathy's face.

"Just rest quiet," Hanrahan said. "Rest quiet."

But Abernathy went on anyway.

"I had to leave the castle, Mrs. Weller. Don't you see I could never prove that I was a man if I stayed there?"

By now, the meaning of Abernathy's words had begun to register with Hanrahan.

The RCMP was made up of many types of men, from farm boys to rough seamen with questionable pasts. Nobody really quizzed each other about what they'd done in previous years. Sometimes, indeed, it was best not to know.

But this was the first time Hanrahan had ever heard of British royalty running away from home and joining the Mounties.

The whole notion perplexed Hanrahan. Why would somebody who had a castle to live in, and servants to wait on him, and fair damsels to choose from trade all that to spend his time in the Canadian version of the Outback, acrawl with Indians, gunners, whiskey runners, and every known description of con man, thief, and killer?

But then he thought of Abernathy's own words: "I could never prove that I was a man if I stayed there."

Hanrahan glanced around to see if anybody else had come awake yet.

This was not knowledge the young Abernathy would want spread around. No, sir; poor boys, which was what many of the Mounties were, would have no sympathy for a lord, even though Abernathy seemed like a decent and modest fellow.

And then Abernathy's eyes came open and there in the moonlight he stared up at Hanrahan.

"How'm I doing?"

"You're doing fine."

"You sure?"

"I'm sure."

Hanrahan could see the fear in Abernathy's eyes.

"Did I talk much?" Abernathy said.

"A little."

Abernathy studied the other man hard now. "Anything important?"

"I guess not."

Hanrahan knew what this felt like. When you got drunk the night before, you sometimes awoke in the morning to wonder what secrets you'd divulged to others. Panic and embarrassment often set in.

But Abernathy was not a dope. "You know, don't you?"

"Know what?" Hanrahan thought by playing dumb he could change the subject.

"The truth about me."

Hanrahan quickly scanned the sleeping men. "I wouldn't say any more right now if I was you, Abernathy."

"You going to tell them?"

"Don't see no reason to."

"You promise?"

"I promise."

"You know what they'd be like if they found out."

"I know."

"You're a good friend, Hanrahan, and I mean it."

"You rest now."

"That sounds like a good idea." Then he paused and said, "There's something else, Hanrahan."

And he then told Hanrahan about trying to catch and trap Carmichael. "I should've told Sergeant Adams when I first started suspecting Carmichael."

Hanrahan nodded. "Yes, you should've." He smiled. "Next time you'll know better. Now rest."

And moments later, Abernathy was sleeping again.

Once he'd checked the dressings, making sure they were in proper position, Hanrahan stood up and walked out to the edge of the camp. He took out the makings and rolled himself a cigarette, an impressive figure in his red coat there in the moonlight.

Yes, his father would definitely be impressed with him tonight—showing off his medical skills as he had, and befriending a genuine British lord.

David Adams found the pit with little trouble. The stench alone guided him to it. He saw his brother lashed to it and crawled slowly to his feet, checking around for any onlookers.

The people at the front, fortunately, busied themselves shooting at the Indians who had appeared, then vanished.

Once on his feet, David made straight for the pit, passing empty lean-tos and darkened cabins.

Dogs roamed the yard and yipped at him but in all the commotion nobody took note.

He came up from behind his brother. He worked around to the front of the pit. The garbage that filled the small, circular hole made him gag. He wondered how Frank had stood it this long.

When Frank saw him, he was smart and said nothing.

David flashed his knife. Frank nodded.

David returned to the back of the pit and started slicing through his brother's rawhide bonds.

He got the hands free with little difficulty.

The legs were another problem. For one thing, David had to lean on the edge of the pit, his face very near the garbage and feces that filled it. By now, the stench was overpowering. He wondered if he shouldn't stop and make himself vomit. Maybe he'd feel better if he did.

But after sucking air into his lungs several times, he was ready again to lean forward and resume work.

Even without the smell, the rawhide wrapped around Frank's legs would have been tough. The rawhide had dug into the denim of Frank's jeans and was knotted up in several places from where Frank had tried to kick free.

Finally, David had some success.

He had just cut through the first layer of the rawhide when Frank shouted, "You'd better watch out, brother."

David peeked around the post and saw a huge, wild, black-haired man running toward the pit. The man was dressed like a trapper and carried a knife that looked like a small sword. Even from here, David could see that the knife was stained with blood.

David jumped to his feet.

Dizzy from the odors, he careened around the pit, positioning himself to meet the larger man.

From somewhere inside his fur jacket, the wild man drew a revolver. Now both his hands were full.

David started to draw his own revolver but the larger man shot the gun from David's hand.

David's fingers stung. The smell of gunsmoke now joined the other acrid odors.

The wild man waved his knife in the air, signaling for David to take out his own weapon.

Which David did, even though his hunch was that this man was far more proficient with a blade than David would ever be.

The man began circling.

David started circling, too.

Each taking his stock of the other, the men started looking for first advantage.

The wild man made the first move.

He jumped forward at David, slashing a button off the Mountie's red coat.

The big man laughed with almost idiotic glee.

"He's going to tear you apart, Dubois," Frank called from

his post. He said this as he began to work his legs free from the last of their bindings. It would take a few minutes but he knew he could get it done.

David almost smiled. He wished he had his brother's confidence that he was going to beat Dubois here.

Dubois went back to circling.

The next move belonged to David. Dubois started to stumble and David lunged forward to slash the edge of his blade across Dubois's face.

The wild man screamed in pain.

Cutting him this way gave David a little more self-confidence. Maybe he wasn't as rusty with a blade as he'd feared.

But then Dubois tilted the contest the other way, lashing out unexpectedly with his right leg and knocking David off his feet.

David landed on his back on the hard ground.

Dubois wasted no time. He dove straight for the fallen Mountie, his outsize knife blade pointed directly at David's heart.

David rolled away just in time.

Dubois scrambled to his feet and tried to tackle the Mountie but David managed to get to his own feet and turn around, facing Dubois only inches away.

With his free hand, David landed a resounding blow on the trapper's jaw.

Dubois was clearly jarred. He went staggering backward, his arms flailing for balance.

David wasted no time.

Now, he kicked up with the steel toe of his long, polished boot, catching Dubois square in the groin.

The wild man let out an ever wilder yell, so loud this time that people at the front of the stockade finally heard him and came running back.

At first, the people who showed up looked as if they were going to grab David and hold him for Dubois to kill but Frank shouted, "Let them fight fair and square!"

One thing the stockade folks liked was violence, particularly when they could just be spectators.

So they arrayed themselves in a semicircle and watched the rest of the contest.

Dubois, limping slightly from being kicked so hard in the groin, regained his composure anyway.

He started circling again, his blade ready once more.

Fury made him even uglier than usual.

David had no doubt that if the man got half a chance, he would kill the Mountie in the slowest and most painful way possible.

Dubois startled David by very accurately hurling his blade directly into David's chest.

David knew instantly that he was badly wounded. The blood flow was already furious.

And then Dubois, taunting him as he did so, reached in and jerked his knife free from David's chest.

David could do nothing to stop Dubois. The shock to his system from the wound had weakened him, made him groggy.

Now Dubois began talking to him in French Canadian curses, only a few of which David recognized. But the tone of the wild man's voice said it all.

Dubois began playing with the seriously weakened David. The crowd cheered Dubois on.

Dubois reached up and flicked David's Mountie Stetson off, trampling it in the dust to the delight of the crowd.

All David could do was stagger around.

Then Dubois began slashing off buttons from David's proud red coat.

Dubois's laughter filled David's ears.

And then, knowing this was his last best chance, David decided to return the favor.

He would hurl his own knife into Dubois.

If he missed, Dubois would certainly kill him. But it looked as if he were a dead man anyway.

He had nothing to lose.

Trying to still his swirling head, trying to half close one eye to steady his aim, David raised his arm despite the pain in his chest and began circling Dubois.

Frank's yell of encouragement, while mostly drowned out

by the crowd, nonetheless sounded good to David. At the same time, Frank felt the last of his bonds work free from his legs.

Dubois was circling again, too, just toying with David and enjoying himself immensely.

"Kill that Mountie sonofabitch!" a particularly loud man in the crowd yelled.

"Kill 'im so I can git his purty red jacket to wear!" giggled another man.

Every few moments, some of the little kids who had joined their parents in watching the fight sailed rocks at David's back.

But he had no time to worry about rocks.

He had to prepare himself to hurl his knife.

And then he stumbled and fell to one knee. The blood loss was making him weak.

He wondered if he could stand up again. Maybe he'd fall over backward in the dust and Dubois would kill him now.

He saw Dubois raise his leg, ready to kick David in the face.

Somehow David found the strength to get his face away from Dubois's boot in time, and to force himself to his feet once again.

Several people in the crowd made derisive comments about Dubois's failure to kick David.

A couple of the little kids called him names.

Angered, Dubois once again started circling.

From the renewed rage in his eyes, it was clear that he was through fooling with David.

He was now coming in for the kill.

Once more, David started to raise his knife hand.

The pain from his wound almost blacked him out.

Must. Raise. Arm.

Must. Throw. Soon.

And so he did.

Just as the knife arced in the air, the crowd started screaming for Dubois to see it.

But he had gotten out of the way too late.

The knife landed true, right in the center of his left eye, blinding him instantly and inflicting even more pain than he'd put on David.

The crowd roared, happy that somebody—anybody—had been so violently injured.

And then David joined Dubois there on the ground, the black tide coming up and rolling over him and taking him down, down.

chapter
twenty-three

FRANK BOLTED FROM THE PIT AS THE CROWD
started gathering around the fallen Dubois.

He ran over to his brother, picked him up, and slung him
over his back. He also snatched up David's gun belt and
revolver.

Now all Frank could think of was getting his brother
to safety before the people of the stockade saw them and
moved in on them.

But already it was too late.

Barton Jaeger, running back here from the front, saw
them and started yelling for someone to stop them.

Gunshots cracked across the night air.

Frank hurried to a corner of the stockade where he could
set his wounded brother behind a water trough and where
they could both take momentary cover.

Frank had just knelt down behind the trough, laying out
his brother and making him as comfortable as possible, when
the gunplay started in earnest.

Bullets sang and sizzled past his head.

The familiar stench of gunfire filled Frank's nostrils.

As he was crouched down behind the trough, he saw
somebody crawling over the top of the timber at the rear
of the stockade.

A sentry. He was just a few yards away.

Frank spun around, filling his hand with David's Deana
and Adams long-barreled revolver, and opened fire.

He caught the sentry clean in the chest.

The man made a gargling sound—blood already filling

his throat—and then fell backward.

But the circle of people firing at him from the yard gave Frank no rest at all.

They kept volley after volley coming.

Frank wished he had time to check on David and see how his younger brother was doing but he knew that was impossible for now.

Besides, he had a mission.

He wanted to crawl back to where the sentry lay and get the man's carbine. That would come in damn handy right now.

He turned around and got flat on his belly and began the three-yard crawl to the sentry.

Bullets spanged off rock and timber. Shouts went up to rush the trough and take him out but Frank knew that they would be careful. They would certainly get him if they rushed the trough but several of them would die in the process.

He reached the sentry.

The man was still in the final moments of life, his body twitching grotesquely as his soul prepared to flee.

Frank got his carbine, then started searching in the man's pockets for extra bullets. He found a sizable handful in the left front pocket.

The man moaned, still not quite ready to die.

Frank did him a favor. He raised the handle of his revolver and brought it crushing down on the side of his head. The man moaned once more and then was silent.

The man was dead for sure now.

Frank turned around and crawled back to the trough.

The first thing Louise Weller heard was the gunfire.

She just hoped she was not too late.

She lashed her horse faster, faster to the stockade.

The carbine was a considerable help to Frank. It also gave him a certain rough pleasure.

Killing somebody with a revolver was one thing but watching them drop from a carbine was another.

While the people in the yard had dragged forth a variety of things to hide behind, setting up a small stockade wall right in the center of the yard, every once in a while one of them would pop up like a clay bird in a shooting gallery and Frank would let go with the carbine.

He was awfully good with the carbine and the stockade people came to know this quickly.

He didn't see Barton Jaeger anywhere in the fighting, which disappointed him. Frank hadn't forgotten that he'd come to the stockade in the first place to kill the man who'd killed his father.

Just now, he shot another man, exploding the center of his forehead.

Even above the gunfire, you could hear the guy screaming his way down into the deep pit of death.

Below him, David moaned.

"Frank."

Frank ducked even closer to his brother.

"Frank, give me a pistol."

"You're too weak to shoot."

"I'll be all right."

"You've lost a lot of blood."

David grinned weakly. "I'll lose even more if they get back here and get their hands on me."

Frank grinned back. "I guess you've got a point there, brother."

And with that, he handed David the revolver.

Getting up for David wasn't easy. It happened in slow, painful stages and several times he had to stop and wait for the dizziness to subside before he could continue.

But finally he made it to the edge of the trough. He took his place for firing and then let go just as a particularly drunken man was starting to rush from the yard toward the trough.

David shot him in the arm.

"Still a Mountie." Frank grinned. It was a long-running joke between them. U.S. lawmen tended to shoot to kill. Mounties, ever the good guys of law enforcement, shot to wound.

"Still a Mountie," David said.

Then another volley of shots started and David and Frank Adams found themselves quite busy.

"Corporal McKenzie?"

"Yes, Hanrahan."

"He's better now."

"Thank you for working on him."

"Yessir."

They stood on the hill looking out over the winding silver ribbon of river and the deep pine forest.

"Corporal McKenzie?"

"Yes, Hanrahan."

"You want to go, don't you?"

"Go?"

"Yessir. To the stockade."

"Yes, I suppose I do."

"So do I. I hate to leave Sergeant Adams all alone like that."

"We'll figure it out, Hanrahan."

"Yessir, I imagine we will."

When Louise reached the stockade, she saw Quanto and his men sitting in the shadows, watching the gun battle.

Her first reaction was fear. Indians, even those living under treaty, were not to be trusted.

But Quanto said, "Don't be afraid, white woman. I'm helping the Mountie named Adams."

And then he explained everything that had happened.

"You have to ride back and get the rest of the patrol and have them come here fast," she said.

Quanto looked surprised and then ashamed that he hadn't thought of this.

He nodded.

In moments, Quanto and his men were on their horses and fleeing into the moonlit night.

Louise went on foot into the stockade in search of Barton Jaeger.

chapter twenty-four

BROTHER EDMUND SAW THE ADULTERESS sneaking through the stockade gate and he knew that at last the Lord had given him a chance to regain His good graces.

Brother Edmund had stayed in his cabin during the gunfire, sitting in a small circle of his brothers and sisters as a plump woman with crazed red hair took a field mouse and slit open its belly and then passed along the entrails for the others to eat.

Brother Edmund had eaten his share but no more. A full stomach made you groggy.

Prayers were offered then, and one of the brothers went into his description of the vision he had had last night. His visions were frequent and quite dull.

Brother Edmund had decided to have a peek outside and that was when he saw the Weller woman and knew that his chance for redemption had come at last.

He eased his way out of the shadows, watched carefully where she was going, and hastened after her.

Meanwhile, the gun battle went on uninterrupted.

Once he was sure where Louise Weller was going, Brother Edmund snuck back to his own cabin momentarily.

He woke his sleeping wife.

She still cried each night over their dead child.

In the darkness, her breath smelled of bad teeth and dead meat.

He said. "The Lord has given us a chance to avenge our dead child."

"And how is that, Brother Edmund?"

"The adulteress is here."

"In the stockade?"

"Yes."

"Now?"

"Yes."

"Oh, God is just, God is good," she said.

"I will repay her. Don't worry."

He leaned over and took his wife's hand and squeezed it. "Your womb will bear the fruit of the Lord again, I will see to it."

"God is just, God is good."

"I will be back soon," Brother Edmund said.

He got up and made his way carefully to the door.

Soon he was outside, and in shadow, and watching Barton Jaeger's cabin.

"How you doing, brother?" Frank called to David.

"Holding up, I guess."

Frank looked at David's thoroughly soaked red coat. The blood loss had been incredible. The kid's guts and stamina were astonishing.

As if greatly irritated at brother David's sorry condition, Frank turned back to the gun battle and promptly shot a man in the shoulder. Then for good measure he put a clean shot right through the bastard's heart as well.

"Good shooting," David said. "I just wish all this killing wasn't necessary."

Frank laughed. "I finally start having a good time and you turn into an old maid."

Louise didn't knock.

She just pushed on inside to Barton Jaeger's dark cabin.

Apparently, over the blazing guns, he didn't hear her come in.

She watched him for a time.

He was packing two large carpetbags. He obviously meant to clear out and fast.

She stepped on a loose floorboard.

The noise spun him around. A .45 filled his hand. He had it pointed directly at her chest.

"My God," he said, "I could have killed you."

There was no mistaking the look and sound of him—he was still painfully in love with her.

She wondered how a man capable of such deep love could have snuck into Fort Cree and murdered an old man in his sleep.

Handsome and charming as he was, Jaeger was not a man she'd ever come to know or understand.

And then he took three huge steps to her and drew her forcefully into his embrace.

He made tiny whimpering sounds of joy.

She wanted to push him away—she felt more than ever like the "whore" her husband had accused her of being—but she knew for now she'd have to pretend to still love him.

"I was coming to get you tonight," he said, turning from her and pointing to the carpetbags. "I thought we could get to a port in a few days and then sail for Europe. I've got several bank accounts there."

His eyes searched her face for an answer.

"I need to ask you something first," she said, suddenly realizing how she could put it to him. "I need you to let Frank and David Adams go."

He looked confused, almost hurt. "What're you talking about? They came here to kill me."

"Don't you think I feel anything for my husband? David is his best friend. If I go away with you, I want to leave him something, someone—If you spared their lives, it would make it a lot easier for me to run away with you."

He eyed her skeptically. "Then you'll go with me?"

She nodded. "If you let the brothers go."

"And if I don't?"

She turned her head back to the door. "Then I go back home and tell my husband that his best friend has been killed."

He didn't know if he believed her or not but he was so exhilarated by her presence that he had no choice but to go along with things.

"You know how much I've missed you?"

She knew he wanted her to respond so she said, "I've missed you, too."

"You've thought about me?"

"All the time."

"Don't lie to me, Louise."

"I'm not lying."

He took her in his arms again. "Louise."

"What?"

He tried to see her better in the dark, tried to discern if she was telling him the truth.

There was a kind of madness to all this, knowing that she might well be deceiving him for her own purposes but also knowing that he wanted her to deceive him.

He loved her too much to want the truth—if the truth was bad.

"You'll like Europe."

"I'm sure I will."

"Wait till you see the restaurants in Rome."

"You'll let them go?"

He hesitated. "I just wish you sounded more enthusiastic. There's something in your voice that just doesn't seem—"

She put a tender finger to his lips. "You're afraid, Barton. That's all. You're afraid that it's not going to come true but it is. I promise."

She angled them slightly toward the door.

"Now go out there and tell those people to quit shooting at David and his brother. Will you do that please?"

He shrugged. He had to play his hand out. He slid his arm through hers.

"Walk out with me. I don't want to let you go even for this little bit."

There was something pathetic about seeing a man as case-hardened as Jaeger being sappy this way.

"You can do it by yourself, Barton. You're a big boy."

He leaned in and kissed her on the lips. "You're quite a woman, Louise. Quite a woman."

And with that, he walked outside his cabin, into the blazing gun battle.

Quanto's horse was sweating badly by the time he reached the Mountie camp.

Quanto told them in broken English what was going on and how badly the Adams brothers needed them.

Within moments, the Mounties were saddling up.

McKenzie led them, of course. He told himself that it was not proper that he felt so good about this. After all, men might lose their lives just so he could play soldier.

But no matter how hard he tried, he could not keep from feeling exhilaration.

He waved his men onward toward the stockade.

"How many you think I've bagged so far?" Frank Adams said, ducking a bullet.

"Maybe ten."

"Hell, I'll bet I've bagged fifteen."

"Just like a U.S. lawman. Always bragging."

Frank peeked up over the trough and let two bullets fly from his carbine.

"Make that sixteen," he said, ducking down again after killing yet another man. He smiled at his brother.

Peeking around the corner of the trough, moving carefully because of his dizziness, David said, "Guess who's joining in."

"Who?"

"Jaeger."

"I just want one shot at the sonofabitch," Frank said, all the bitterness and frustration over his father's death clear in his voice.

"Something's going on."

"What?"

"Don't know. He's walking up to the front of the crowd."

Frank eased his head up above the trough so he could get a better look at Jaeger.

• • •

Jaeger got to the front of the crowd and started firing his own pistol in the air.

At first, several of the stockade people kept firing at the trough but Jaeger eventually got their attention.

"I want to talk to you people. There's been a change in plans."

Reluctantly, they stopped shooting as Jaeger turned toward the trough. "Adams—you listen to this, too."

"What the hell's going on here?" Frank wanted to know. But he listened.

Brother Edmund eased open the door leading into Jaeger's cabin and moved his way into the interior darkness.

At first, he did not see the woman at all, not even the outline of her.

But then she moved toward the front and his eyes rested on her.

She was beautiful, with a graceful body clearly made for sin. There was no doubt she was the devil's tool. There was no doubt she had caused the death of his daughter.

"Who are you?" Louise Weller said.

He almost laughed.

Even without knowing exactly who he was, she was frightened. She had a sense of how God's wrath was working through him. And how that wrath would soon enough be visited on her.

"You destroyed my daughter."

"What?"

"You heard me, harlot."

"I don't even know who you are."

"Yes, you do. In your heart you know who I am."

"Please leave or I'll call Barton."

"It's too late for Barton. He was the one who brought sin down on this stockade and now he must pay by losing the one he loves the same way I lost my daughter."

"No, please, I—"

She was starting to retreat into the shadows, putting her hands over her face, trying to find the power to scream in a dry and constricted throat—

—when he raised the knife—

—plunged it deep between her bountiful breasts.

She screamed now but even so it was not a sound that would carry past the cabin door.

He ripped the knife free again, raised it dripping above his head, and then began stabbing her in a series of frenzied movements that she was powerless to do anything about.

"You killed my daughter, harlot!" he cried over and over. "You killed my daughter!"

She had one last burst of strength left and in her dying, she used it.

She clawed her nails across his face and then pushed him into Jaeger's desk so hard that he went over backward, striking the back of his head against the desktop.

For a moment his head swam and he felt his fingers losing their grip on the hilt of his knife.

She pushed past him then, and out the cabin door, staggering into the torchlight of the yard where the stockade people had gathered listening to Jaeger.

Somebody shouted when they first saw her and then Jaeger, who had just told his people that he wanted Frank and David Adams to be set free, turned and saw the woman he loved staggering from the cabin.

At first, he hardly recognized her. Her chest and face had been so hacked up that she looked to be wearing a bloody costume of some kind.

But then he heard her sobbing and calling for help and he rushed to her.

The stockade people stood around and watched as Jaeger took the dying woman in his arms and laid her gently on the ground, pillowing her head with his arm.

"I love you, Louise. I love you."

But if she understood his words, she did not respond to them. Her lovely eyes seemed fixed on some point in the starry sky, some restful place she would soon visit perhaps.

"Who did this to you? Who, Louise?" Jaeger's voice was now frantic, crazed.

And then he raised his head and saw Brother Edmund emerging from the cabin.

Brother Edmund was soaked with blood.

And then Jaeger remembered the man's crazy words about Jaeger's adulterous affair bringing the Lord's wrath down on the stockade and how the Lord had taken Brother Edmund's daughter in vengeance.

Jaeger looked back at Louise and realized that in the few moments he'd looked away she had died.

"Louise," he said, tears filling his eyes.

He put her head gently to the ground and then slowly stood up to face Brother Edmund who was scurrying across the edge of his yard to his own cabin.

Everybody in the stockade knew what was about to happen. Brother Edmund had killed the woman Barton Jaeger loved. Now he was about to pay for his transgression.

Watching all this, just as horrified and as fascinated as the onlookers, Frank Adams whispered to David, "Now's my chance."

"To do what?"

"Just sit here, brother, and let me take care of it."

And with that, Frank Adams got up on his haunches and started crawling out from behind the water trough, circling wide along the periphery of the stockade. Nobody noticed him. Everybody was too busy watching Jaeger and Brother Edmund.

"You killed her."

"She brought sin and wrath down upon this stockade."

"She was a defenseless woman."

"She was a tainted harlot."

Slowly, Jaeger drew his revolver from his holster. "I should have killed you a long time ago."

"I'm not afraid of death. Others will carry on my work. That is all that matters."

"You killed her," Jaeger said again, still sounding as if he could not bring himself to believe this simple fact.

And then he started firing.

The shots were loud in the still night, three, four, five shots.

Brother Edmund soon crumpled down into death.

Jaeger stood several feet from him, his revolver still smoking, when Frank Adams ran up behind him and put his own weapon dead against the back of Jaeger's head.

"I'd like to do the same thing to you that you just did to Brother Edmund," Frank said. "So I'd remember that if I were you."

If Jaeger was impressed with Frank's words, he certainly didn't let on.

"Let you take me back to the fort so I can be tried and hanged," Jaeger said. "No, thanks."

"You've got one bullet left. Maybe you'll get lucky."

"That's how I've lived my life," Jaeger said. "Based on luck."

And with that, he spun away from Frank and dropped down to fire his last remaining bullet.

Frank had hoped for this, of course, so he was ready for it.

He pumped three shots into Jaeger's chest before the other man could even squeeze off his last wild shot.

Soon Jaeger lay dying, stretched out in the dust.

Several of the stockade people were obviously thinking of taking some shots of their own at Frank but they were quickly dissuaded by the sight of the Mountie patrol bursting through the front gates of the stockade, with Corporal James K. McKenzie proudly leading the charge.

Without a single shot being fired, McKenzie and his men rounded up and disarmed the stockade people and began searching their cabins and lean-tos for anybody who might be hiding.

It was in one such cabin that they found their old friend

Carmichael, who had betrayed everything sacred to the Mounties, quivering in the shadows.

"You're a disgrace to that coat," McKenzie said, and slapped the man across the face.

Then he personally put Carmichael in handcuffs.

chapter
twenty-five

ON THE SLOPE OF A HILL FOUR HUNDRED YARDS west of the entrance to Fort Cree stood a cross with the name INSPECTOR ADAMS burned into the wood.

In the soft spring wind, hands folded in front of them, heads downcast and eyes closed, brothers David and Frank Adams said silent prayers for their father.

Both men believed that somehow their father knew that they had avenged his murder, and was proud of them.

Soon, they put their hats back on and returned to Fort Cree, making their way among the merchants and Crees and travelers who chose to make camp on the grassy slopes outside the fort.

"You going to see Robert again soon?" Frank said, referring to Louise's husband.

"Thought I would."

"He took it pretty hard."

On their way back to Fort Cree from Jaeger's stockade, the patrol had stopped by Robert Weller's cabin. David had gone inside and told the man that his wife was dead. His story was that she had been upset over their argument and had gone for a ride. Jaeger's people had kidnapped her and taken her back to the stockade and to Jaeger. David had said nothing about the relationship between the man and the woman. Weller, drunk as always, had fallen into violent sobbing. All David could do was sit silently and watch. And then Weller said a curious thing: "I want you to take every whiskey bottle up there and smash it for me."

"You sure, Robert?"

179

"That's the least I can do for her, isn't it?"

And so David had complied, using the handle of his Enfield revolver to smash a half-dozen whiskey bottles, leaving a wooden box filled with jagged pieces of glass and a stench of whiskey that wafted out across the yard.

"You going to be all right?" David had asked.

All Robert had done was start quietly crying again. Knowing that now was a good time to leave his friend alone, David had returned to his patrol and they'd headed back to the fort.

Tomorrow morning Carmichael would be bound over in shackles and sent to Mountie headquarters in Regina where he would be tried on several serious charges.

It was just dawn as the brothers entered the fort now. Reveille had sounded half an hour ago and the day was just beginning to take form, the shouts of men hurrying to turn out at 7:15 A.M., followed soon by breakfast; of horses just waking in the stables; of the blacksmith already clanging out his daily tasks; of young men of various nationalities running, running everywhere as they tugged on their smart red jackets that they wore with unmistakable pride.

David looked at it all fondly. He enjoyed the military atmosphere of this very special police force.

He was thinking this as he reached the stable where Frank's bay was already saddled and waiting.

Frank was different, of course, David thought. A loner. Give him a six-pointed star and a badge. That was the only "military atmosphere" Frank ever needed or wanted.

Frank swung up into the saddle, steadying the bay.

"There'll never be another one like him," Frank said, looking down at his brother.

"No, there won't."

"He was the best damn old man a couple of brothers like us could ever want."

"He sure was, Frank."

Neither man wanted to acknowledge the lumps that had caught in their throats, so Frank just looked down, put the edge of his right hand against the brim of his white Stetson in a small salute, and said, "You know, brother, you're a hell of a good guy."

"Funny thing," David said. "I was just about to say the same about you."

"You going to keep in touch?"

"You bet."

Frank nodded to his younger brother and said, "You look more like the old man every day. In that uniform, I mean."

"I take that as a high compliment."

Frank smiled. "That's the way I meant it."

Then Frank spurred his mount and rode out of Fort Cree.

David walked behind him all the way to the front gates. Frank didn't turn around and wave good-bye. He just kept riding, which was just like Frank.

David had just started thinking about the old man again when somebody said, "Sir, I want to report a possible infraction of the rules in the barracks."

David turned to find his least favorite apple-polisher Johansen standing there.

"You do, eh?" David said, laughing out loud. Things were getting back to normal again around here and David was most appreciative.

"What is it this time, Johansen," David said as he escorted the recruit back to the barracks. "One of the men belch out loud at breakfast?"

Johansen had the good grace to blush. But he persisted. "No, sir, some of the men were actually gambling for money last night."

Sergeant Adams looked at recruit Johansen and said, "I'm sure glad we have you to keep us on the straight and narrow. You know that, Johansen?"

Then he and the recruit walked over to mess for breakfast.

If you enjoyed this book, subscribe now and get...

TWO FREE

A $7.00 VALUE—

If you would like to read more of the very best, most exciting, adventurous, action-packed Westerns being published today, you'll want to subscribe to True Value's Western Home Subscription Service.

Each month the editors of True Value will select the 6 very best Westerns from America's leading publishers for special readers like you. You'll be able to preview these new titles as soon as they are published, *FREE* for ten days with no obligation!

TWO FREE BOOKS

When you subscribe, we'll send you your first month's shipment of the newest and best 6 Westerns for you to preview. With your first shipment, two of these books will be yours as our introductory gift to you absolutely *FREE* (a $7.00 value), regardless of what you decide to do. If

you like them, as much as we think you will, keep all six books but pay for just 4 at the low subscriber rate of just $2.75 each. If you decide to return them, keep 2 of the titles as our gift. No obligation.

Special Subscriber Savings

When you become a True Value subscriber you'll save money several ways. First, all regular monthly selections will be billed at the low subscriber price of just $2.75 each. That's at least a savings of $4.50 each month below the publishers price. Second, there is never any shipping, handling or other hidden charges—*Free home delivery*. What's more there is no minimum number of books you must buy, you may return any selection for full credit and you can cancel your subscription at any time. A TRUE VALUE!

A special offer for people who enjoy reading the best Westerns published today.

WESTERNS!

NO OBLIGATION

Mail the coupon below

To start your subscription and receive 2 FREE WESTERNS, fill out the coupon below and mail it today. We'll send your first shipment which includes 2 FREE BOOKS as soon as we receive it.

Mail To: **True Value Home Subscription Services, Inc. P.O. Box 5235 120 Brighton Road, Clifton, New Jersey 07015-5235**

YES! I want to start reviewing the very best Westerns being published today. Send me my first shipment of 6 Westerns for me to preview FREE for 10 days. If I decide to keep them, I'll pay for just 4 of the books at the low subscriber price of $2.75 each; a total $11.00 (a $21.00 value). Then each month I'll receive the 6 newest and best Westerns to preview Free for 10 days. If I'm not satisfied I may return them within 10 days and owe nothing. Otherwise I'll be billed at the special low subscriber rate of $2.75 each; a total of $16.50 (at least a $21.00 value) and save $4.50 off the publishers price. There are never any shipping, handling or other hidden charges. I understand I am under no obligation to purchase any number of books and I can cancel my subscription at any time, no questions asked. In any case the 2 FREE books are mine to keep.

Name			
Street Address			Apt. No.
City	State		Zip Code
Telephone			
Signature			

(If under 18 parent or guardian must sign)

Terms and prices subject to change. Orders subject to acceptance by True Value Home Subscription Services, Inc.

13076